SENIOR YEAR SURPRISE

SENIOR YEAR SURPRISE

Quentin A. Terrell

To order additional copies of this book, contact:
Xlibris Corporation
1-888-7-XLIBRIS
www.Xlibris.com
Orders@Xlibris.com

CONTENTS

INTRODUCTION

This is a story that follows two very shy and very popular high school seniors in a suburban city in Mississippi, with dark, lonely childhoods and painful emotional scars, that have the most wonderful Senior year of high school in addition to defying the odds against them and finishing high school.

During the memorable Senior year, the two students are happily dating each other, and most of the students, faculty, and administration at the school see them as a terrific couple, as well as wonderful role models for the lower classes.

Not everyone on the school campus is happy for the two students. During the Spring semester of the school year, six girls that are part of the Freshman class try their best to threaten the students' easygoing Senior year. Despite the setbacks that the two Senior students face, they go on to have the most wonderful Senior year that no high school student has ever had before.

In short, this story focuses on two bright students' successful efforts to have the most wonderful Senior year that no high school student has ever had before.

ONE

Keisha Blackledge was a very shy teenage girl who lived in a small, suburban city named Canaby just outside of Jackson in the state of Mississippi. She was a senior at Canaby High School, and she was very popular there. She was the lead singer of the school choir, a hot item in beauty pageants, the star varsity football cheerleader, and was voted class favorite in previous years.

It was a Friday night in October, 1995, around seven-ten, on the Oakwood City High School campus. Oakwood City, like Canaby, was also a suburb of Jackson. The Canaby Warriors were about to play the Oakwood City Tigers in a non-Region 3-5A football road game that was often referred to as a "Rankin County Rivalry" game. While the stands were full, the school band was practicing on a game song, the dance team members, called the "Dream Daisies," were in the top part of the stands, just above the band, and there were lots of football fans, as well as high school students, all over the place. The concession stands at the football game were almost ready.

But when Keisha and her boyfriend, David Malone, arrived at the football field, they had only one thing on their minds: their love for each other. David was not having a very good day.

"David, aren't you glad to be at this football game?" asked Keisha, "and to see me cheer?"

"I guess," said David. "At least this can help me make up for what happened today."

"David, don't feel bad about it," said Keisha.

"Well, thanks for telling me that," said David.

"I tell you what," said Keisha, "why don't we do something wonderful tomorrow night? Just to get away from the stressful week that both of us have had."

"That sounds great," said David.

Just then a dance team member named Courtney arrived at the football game. She was best friends with David, and they had a class together.

"Hey David?" she asked. "Are you feeling better?"

"Not really," said David.

"I'm sure you'll get over it, David," said Keisha.

"Keisha, maybe you don't understand why he's frustrated," said Courtney. "See, we got our twenty-question quiz grades back today, and no one did good on it. Even David and I had low scores on it."

"But did you two pass it?" asked Keisha.

"Yes," said Courtney. "We had passing grades on the quiz."

"Well, that's no big deal," said Keisha.

"I just hope it doesn't affect my average," said David.

"Don't worry about it, David," said Keisha. "Okay?"

"Okay," said David.

Around seven-thirty, the Canaby football players, coming from the fieldhouse, were headed to the stadium. They were getting ready to run through a large poster that said, "Go, Warriors." Keisha and the rest of the cheerleaders were in front of the poster. When the football players ran through the poster, the cheerleaders started cheering, the band began playing, and everyone on the visiting side of the stadium began applauding. But when the Oakwood City team ran through their poster, which said, "No. 1 Tigers," and their cheerleaders cheered, everyone on the home side began applauding.

When the game started, the Oakwood City team kicked the ball off to the Canaby team, and the two teams played very hard. In the stands on the visiting side, the crowd began cheering the Canaby team on, but David was just watching the game. He was seated in the stands next to the Dream Daisies when they started noticing him. There were 36 dance team members in all.

"Hey, what's wrong with David?" asked a dance team member.

"He might be depressed," said another member. "I heard he's depressed most of the time."

"David's not depressed," said Courtney. "He just had a bad episode this morning, and he's trying to get over it."

At that moment David reacted.

"Hey, I am not depressed," said David.

"Well, we were just wondering," said a third member.

"We're just glad you're okay," said a fourth member.

Just then Courtney and several dance team members sat down beside David to keep him company.

"Are you enjoying the game?" asked Courtney.

"Yes, Courtney," said David.

"Well, we're glad," said a fifth member. "We want you to have a great time."

Just then Keisha and the other cheerleaders started cheering as a play was being made out on the field. The quarterback for the Canaby team got the ball, and he then threw it to a running back, but a tackle for the Oakwood City team threw him to the ground. The spectators stood in shock.

"I can't believe they did that to him," said a student named Latasha.

A while later, the spectators watched as a running back for the Oakwood City team ran all the way to the end zone to score the first touchdown of the game. The spectators on the Oakwood City side of the stadium cheered at the play, but when the try for the extra point was successful, the spectators on the Canaby side of the stadium stood in shock. The score was seven to zero in favor of Oakwood City, and it was five-twenty-one left in the first quarter.

"Now I know we're going to lose," said a cheerleader.

"I don't think we will." said Keisha. "Anything can happen between Oakwood City and Canaby."

Later at the football game, the lines to both concession stands were long. A concession stand worker on the Canaby side of the stadium was serving a number of students, including Latasha.

"May I help you?" he asked.

"Yes, I would like a Dr. Pepper, please," said Latasha.

"That will be one dollar," said the employee.

She then gave him a dollar bill. The employee then gave Latasha her soda, and she then stood on the steps of the stands, only to see a Canaby running back with the ball get thrown to the ground.

Soon, it was halftime at Tiger Stadium, and the Canaby High School marching band was about to perform. The Dream Daisies were also on the field. The score was thirteen to six, in favor of Oakwood City. Keisha was in the stands talking to David.

"Are you enjoying the game, David?" she asked.

"Well, yes," said David, "but I wish Canaby was in the lead."

"Maybe they'll take the lead in the second half," said Keisha.

Just then the halftime show started and the band started performing. Keisha and David decided to watch the halftime show together. Soon, the dance team performed, and Keisha and David cheered Courtney on, as the dance team members danced to the song that the band was playing.

Later that night, at a fast food drive-in near the school, lots of high school students were enjoying hamburgers and fries. The game was over, and the place was packed. At the drive-in, there were lots of conversations taking place, but Latasha was standing outside the drive-in all by herself. She was waiting for a few friends to arrive at the restaurant. Soon Keisha and David pulled into the parking lot of the drive-in, and got out of their car.

"I can't believe Oakwood City beat us tonight," said David. "Boy, are they a good football team."

"It will be okay," said Keisha. "Besides, think about the bright side. Next Friday is homecoming at Canaby High School."

At that moment they spotted Latasha.

"Latasha, you must be waiting on someone," said Keisha.

"Yes, I am," said Latasha. "I'm waiting on a couple of football guys to meet me here."

"We'll save you a seat in case they don't show up," said David.

"That's sweet of you, David," said Latasha.

Just then Courtney and several dance team members showed up at the restaurant.

"Twenty-three to sixteen," said Courtney. "Can you all believe it?" she then asked.

"I'm just about as shocked as you are, Courtney," said Latasha.

"It's not our fault that we lost tonight," said Keisha. "Oakwood City just has a better team."

"They've got one of the best records in the state," said a dance team member. "Better yet, they won the Mississippi Class 2A high school football championship game in 1991, 1992, 1993, and last year."

"And they've been ranked in the MHSAA Little 10 poll every week since the 1991 season," said a dance team member.

"They're seven and zero overall," said a third dance team member.

"Eight and zero counting tonight's game," said a fourth dance team member.

"It's no wonder we got beat tonight," said David.

"It's not your fault, David," said Latasha.

"I know that," said David.

"We just don't want you blaming yourself for it," said Courtney.

"I'm not blaming myself for it," said David.

A while later, Keisha, David, Latasha, Courtney, her dance team friends, and a lot of cheerleaders all were enjoying burgers and fries, sharing a huge conversation at the same time.

"Did you all know that homecoming is next week?" asked Courtney.

"That's right," said Keisha. "And David and I are the highlight of it all."

"What do you mean by that?" asked Latasha.

"I mean, I'm the homecoming queen," said Keisha, "and David is my escort."

"Latasha, you're coming to see us," said David, "aren't you?"

"Of course I am," said Latasha. "What makes you all think I'm not coming to homecoming?"

"We just want you to see Keisha and David walk the football field," said a dance team member.

"Well, I'm planning to see Keisha and David together in the homecoming ceremonies," said Latasha. "Good luck to the two of you."

"Thank you, Latasha," said Keisha.

"I'm gonna need it," said David.

"No, you're not," said Courtney. "You're going to do just fine."

"But what if I get nervous?" asked David.

"You're not going to get nervous," said another dance team member. "We'll even cheer you on."

"Well, thanks," said David.

Later that night, at David's house in Canaby, David was fast asleep in bed when his sister, Robbie, walked into his room. She was curious about her brother's participation in the Canaby High School homecoming ceremonies.

"Hey David?" she asked.

David then turned his lamp on.

"What is it, Robbie?" asked David.

"Good luck to you and Keisha in the homecoming ceremonies next week," said Robbie.

"Thank you Robbie," said David.

"Do you think some of my classmates from school should come and see the two of you in the homecoming ceremonies?" asked Robbie.

"If they want to," said David, "then I don't have a problem with it."

"I mean, some of my classmates are really looking forward to seeing you and Keisha walk the football field next Friday night," said Robbie.

"Well, thanks for telling me that, Robbie," said David.

"I hope a lot of my classmate friends come to see you and Keisha in the homecoming parade and homecoming football game," said Robbie.

"Well, maybe they will," said David. "At least you'll be there to see me."

"That's right," said Robbie. "I wouldn't miss it for the world."

"Well, okay," said David

"Good night, David," said Robbie.

"Good night, Robbie," said David.

Robbie then left the room, and David then turned his lamp off, and went back to bed. While he was asleep, he was thinking about how much fun it would be to escort his own girlfriend while she was the homecoming queen.

The next week, homecoming was on the minds of lots of students at Canaby High School that were looking forward to Homecoming Friday. Around seven-twenty that morning, David, in his car, was arriving on the school campus. The outside of the school was surrounded with students when David parked his car, and got out. He then went into the school building, which was noisy, and packed with students.

When David got to his locker, he was getting his books for his first period class when a group of girls, along with a student tennis player named Paulette, found him.

"Hi, David," said one girl.

David turned around, and saw all seven girls and Paulette.

"Haven't you all got better things to do?" asked David.

"Yes," said a girl named Jodi, "but we wanna be with you."

Just then David closed his locker.

"Look, I'd love to chat with you all," he said, "but I have a class to go to."

"Well, skip it," said a girl named Brianna.

"You all must be crazy," said David.

Just then David started heading to his class.

"Skip your class and hang out with us," said Jodi.

"Yeah, David," said Brianna. "Skip it just for us."

"Why don't you all skip your classes?" suggested David, "instead of following me around."

David then continued to head to his class.

"We're going to get through to him," said Paulette, "one way or the other."

"Oh yeah," said Jodi. "He's gonna answer to us."

In a debate class, David was paired with a junior named Holly, as part of a class project. Latasha was also in the debate class, along with 45 other students.

"How are you doing, David?" asked Holly.

"Not very good," said David.

"Why?" asked Holly. "What's wrong?"

"I'm just nervous about homecoming," said David, "that's all."

"It'll be okay, David," said Holly.

Just then the tardy bell rang, and the teacher walked in.

"Good morning, everyone," he said. "Today, we continue our group debates. And David, I believe you and Holly are the ones to go first today."

At that moment David and Holly went up to the podiums. David and Holly were doing their debates on ice cream. When they were completely finished, everyone in the class gave them a round of applause.

Later that morning at the snack bar, David and Keisha were enjoying ice cream cones while he was talking to her about his debate.

"How did you do on your debate?" asked Keisha.

"I did wonderful on it," said David. "I got an 'A-plus' on it."

"That's excellent," said Keisha. "I'm very proud of you."

"Thank you, Keisha," said David.

At that moment Holly arrived at the snack bar.

"Hi, David," said Holly. "How are you doing?"

David then introduced Keisha to Holly.

"Keisha, this is my debate partner, Holly Rosenberg," said David. "Holly, this is my girlfriend, Keisha Blackledge."

"It's nice to meet you," said Keisha.

"It's nice to meet you, too," said Holly. "You must be the one that's the homecoming queen for this year."

"Yes, Holly," said Keisha. "That's me. I'm the queen."

"The big day is Friday," said David. "Are you coming?"

"Yes, I'm coming," said Holly. "Can you all excuse me for a minute?"

Holly then went to get some ice cream, while Keisha and David chose to sit at an empty table at the snack bar.

"I hope they have ice cream at the carnival tonight," said David.

"Yeah, me too," said David.

Just then Holly found Keisha and David, and stood by their table.

"David, are you going to the carnival tonight?" she asked.

"Yes, Holly," said David. "Are you coming to see me and Keisha in the homecoming ceremonies?"

"Yes, I am," said Holly.

Just then Latasha, her friend Cheryl, and Cheryl's boyfriend, Ronnie, arrived at the snack bar.

"Isn't that wonderful?" asked Ronnie. "Ice cream at the snack bar."

"I didn't even know the snack bar was selling ice cream," said Cheryl.

"Neither did I," said Latasha, "but David did his debate on this."

"Really?" asked Cheryl.

"Yes," said Latasha. "I even listened to him."

Just then Paulette and her friends arrived at the snack bar.

"Hey, David," said Paulette.

"Have you all been bothering my boyfriend?" asked Keisha.

"We wanna spend time with him," said a girl in the group.

"Don't count on it," said Keisha.

"You know, Paulette," said Latasha, "one day, he's gonna beat the living daylights out of you all."

"Oh, really," said Paulette.

"Yeah," said Latasha, "and when he does, I'm going to be standing there and laughing."

"And then I'll be congratulating her for it," said Cheryl.

"Let's get out of here," said Brianna.

Just then Paulette and her friends left the snack bar.

"See ya, David," said Jodi.

David, feeling insulted, just looked on.

"It will be okay, David," said Ronnie.

"I just hope she knows that I'm not breaking up with Keisha for her," said David.

At that moment Jodi, standing just outside the snack bar, blew a kiss at David, in front of Keisha, Holly, Latasha, her friends, and several other students inside the snack bar that were happy for Keisha and David. As lots of female students outside the snack bar were laughing, David, furious over the whole ordeal, stormed out of the snack bar, and snapped at her. Keisha, Holly, and Latasha restrained him.

"You're going to be sorry you did that to me!" yelled David.

"And wouldn't that be great?" asked Jodi. "For the two of us to start dating each other."

"Yeah, in your dreams!" yelled David.

"David, calm down," said Keisha.

Lots of students inside the snack bar were devastated at what was happening to David.

"It will be okay, David," said Latasha. "I promise."

"Hey, don't forget to let her know when you and Keisha break up," said Brianna.

"Yeah, David," said Jodi. "I'm really looking forward to it."

"Why don't you all leave him alone?" suggested Holly.

Around lunchtime that day, a sad, tearful David was sitting all by himself in an empty classroom on the school campus. He was frustrated because he got picked on in the snack bar, and that he thought he was the cause of the whole ordeal. Just then Cheryl and Latasha walked into the room to talk to him.

"Hey David?" asked Latasha, "are you okay?"

David, with tears in his eyes, saw Latasha and Cheryl.

"Leave me alone," said David.

"Come on, David," said Latasha. "Don't let what happened at the snack bar get you down."

"I don't want to talk about it," said David.

"David, I know you're frustrated about . . . ," said Latasha.

"I don't care," said David, cutting her off. "Now leave."

"Don't punish yourself like this, David," said Cheryl. "What happened this morning wasn't your fault."

"You didn't do anything wrong, David," said Latasha. "They are the ones responsible for what happened this morning. Do you understand?"

"Look, I got hurt at the snack bar," said David, fighting back tears, "both physically and emotionally. You don't know what that feels like."

"David, think about the bright side," said Cheryl, "and how popular you are here at Canaby High School, like being on the Principal's

List and in the National Honor Society, Drug-Ed Council, Students Against Drunk Drivers, and lots of other school clubs."

"And besides, think about the homecoming ceremonies Friday night," said Latasha, "and about how proud the student body is going to be when you escort Keisha on the football field."

"I see where this is going now," said David.

Just then Ronnie and Keisha walked into the classroom.

"David, are you okay?" asked Ronnie.

"I'm fine, Ronnie," said David.

"He should be okay," said Latasha. "We comforted him, and talked to him about the big week."

"That's right," said Keisha. "We do have a big week ahead of us."

"He thinks that he caused the incident in the snack bar," said Cheryl.

"Well, he's wrong," said Ronnie. "It wasn't your fault, David."

"It's okay, Ronnie," said David.

"Keisha, isn't tonight carnival night?" asked Cheryl.

"Yeah," said Keisha.

"Then maybe you and David can make up for the snack bar incident at the carnival tonight," said Ronnie.

"Yeah, Ronnie," said Keisha, "maybe so. Doesn't that sound great, David?"

"Yes, Keisha," said David.

That afternoon at home, David was taking a nap when his phone rang. He immediately answered it. It was Keisha.

"Hello," said David.

"Is David there?" asked Keisha.

"This is him," said David.

"David, I'm calling about the carnival," said Keisha.

"Keisha, I was just about to call you about the carnival," said David. "What time do I need to come and pick you up?"

"I'm taking you, remember?" asked Keisha.

"Oh, that's right," said David.

"Anyway, what time will you be ready?" asked Keisha.

"Well, it's three-thirty now," said David, "so I'd say about six-thirty."

"Well, I'll see you then," said Keisha. "Bye, David."

"Bye, Keisha," said David.

Around seven o' clock that night, at the carnival in Canaby, there were hundreds of fairgoers, among them high school, junior college, and college students, that were enjoying the carnival. Some were playing games on the midway, others were enjoying the rides, and some were even buying refreshments. But when Keisha and David got to the carnival, they were sharing a conversation while looking for a place to talk.

"Aren't you glad this week's homecoming week?" asked Keisha.

"Yes," said David. "I mean, I can't wait to escort you in the homecoming ceremonies."

"That's right," said Keisha. "And that's when most of the student body at Canaby High School is going to see us as a happy couple."

"But suppose we had an extra-special Senior year," said David.

"Like, for me to be prom queen," said Keisha, "and for you to be prom king, and for us to be Senior Class Favorites, and for us to be the Valedictorian and Salutatorian of our class. Is that what you're thinking about?"

"Yes," said David. "Like a 'Senior Year Surprise' for us."

"Well, who knows?" asked Keisha. "Maybe it will happen that way."

"Yes, Keisha," said David. "Maybe it will."

Keisha and David didn't let that possibility stop them from having fun at the carnival that night. They rode several rides, and played games on the midway. Soon Paulette and her friends arrived at the carnival looking for David. Six ninth-grade girls were with Paulette and her friends. They wanted to meet David. In another part of the carnival Latasha and her friends were enjoying ice cream cones. In the back of the carnival, Holly was waiting to ride the carnival spaceship when a senior girl named Kerry ran into her.

"Hi, Holly," she said.

"Oh, hi, Kerry," said Holly. "Have you seen David?"

"I saw him earlier," said Kerry.

"See, he was supposed to meet me here at the carnival," said Holly, "and I haven't seen him yet."

"Well, I'm sure you'll find him," said Kerry.

"Okay," said Holly. "Are you going to ride the spaceship with me?"

"I can't," said Kerry. "I have to go find Jenny."

Holly then kept standing at the waiting line all by herself. When the spaceship stopped and the door opened, a huge crowd was coming out of the spaceship. At that moment Holly went into the spaceship all alone. She felt kind of lonely, mainly because no one else was riding. Soon, the door closed, the spaceship started spinning around, and after a while, it was going so fast that the ledge Holly stood on was raised up.

Meanwhile, at the refreshment booth at the carnival, Keisha and David were enjoying bacon cheeseburgers, fries, and sodas.

"At least now we can start our collection of memories here," said Keisha.

"That's right, Keisha," said David. "We can consider the carnival a part of our Senior year, but I don't think there will be any pictures of the carnival in the yearbook."

"Think about it, David," said Keisha. "We could have the best 'Senior Year Surprise' that no high school student has ever had before."

"Well, if it happens," said David, "at least I wouldn't get all crazy over it."

Just then Paulette, her friends, and the ninth-grade girls showed up at the refreshment booth.

"Hello, David," said Paulette.

"Paulette, if you and your friends came over here to bother David," said Keisha, "you all are wasting your time."

"We wanna holler at him," said Brianna.

"Maybe miss Keisha here is afraid that we're gonna steal her prized possession," said a girl in the group.

"Hey David?" asked a ninth-grade girl, "how would you like to go on a date with us?"

"Dream on," said David.

"How would you like to go on a date with me?" asked Jodi.

"Don't count on it," said Keisha.

"Hey, let's get out of here," said another ninth-grade girl.

Paulette, her friends, and the ninth-grade girls then left the refreshment booth.

"See ya, David," said Jodi.

David was just looking on.

"I feel insulted," said David.

"Don't worry about it, David," said Keisha.

A big 'Senior Year Surprise' awaits Keisha and David, but the biggest surprise Keisha could ever have was if she were to stand the test of time with her love for David, in addition to being the 1995 Homecoming Queen and the 1996 Prom Queen at Canaby High School.

TWO

When it came time for the 1995 homecoming ceremonies at Canaby High School, the whole city of Canaby was decorated with white and blue ribbons. Cars that were passing through the city of Canaby on their way to Jackson and Meridian saw most of the decorations. Some houses near Canaby High School were also showing homecoming spirit by displaying toilet paper in trees and yards. On the Canaby High School premises, the entire campus was decorated. And in front of the football field there was a huge sign displayed that said, "Canaby High School Homecoming."

That Friday morning, in the school gymnasium, the pep rally was in full swing. All of the students were excited about the homecoming ceremonies. The football cheerleaders were cheering, the band was playing, and the Dream Daisies dance team even performed a number. After a while, the principal quieted the crowd down.

"Okay, may I have your attention, please?" he asked. "As all of you know, today is Homecoming Friday. That means that there is going to be a parade at three-thirty this afternoon in downtown Canaby. Our homecoming football game against Lauderdale Creek High School is at seven-thirty tonight. Our queen, Keisha Blackledge, will be crowned at halftime at Warrior Stadium. Make your plans to be part of the fun."

At that moment everyone in the crowd applauded, and the principal then turned the pep rally over to the assistant principal so she could announce the homecoming court.

"At this time, I would like to announce our homecoming court for this year," said the assistant principal.

Just then the first homecoming maid and her escort walked into the gymnasium to be introduced.

"This is Freshman maid Chiara Patterson," said the assistant principal, "and her escort, Jason Murphy."

At that moment the Freshman maid and her escort waved at everyone in the auditorium, and they applauded.

"Chiara is a straight-A student, a member of the Dream Daisies dance team," said the assistant principal, "and this year, she was voted class favorite. Jason is a straight-A student, a baseball player here at Canaby High School, and a member of the Student Council. Chiara is the daughter of Rodney and Krista Patterson, and Jason is the son of Mr. and Mrs. Steve Murphy."

Just then the next maid and her escort walked into the gym.

"This is Sophomore maid Kim Lewis," said the assistant principal, "and her escort, Chad Hicks."

The Sophomore maid and her escort waved, and everyone in the auditorium applauded.

"Kim is a straight-A student," said the assistant principal, "a member of the Dream Daisies dance team, a member of the Student Council, and a member of the Vocational and Industrial Clubs of America. Chad is a straight-A student, a member of the Drama club, and is a football player here at Canaby High School. Kim is the daughter of Mr. and Mrs. Frank Lewis, and Chad is the son of Mr. and Mrs. Robert Hicks."

Just then the next maid and her escort walked into the gym.

"This is Junior maid Trina Sands," said the assistant principal, "and her escort, Wayne McGuire."

The Junior maid and her escort waved, and everyone applauded.

"Trina is a straight-A student," said the assistant principal, "a member of the Future Business Leaders of America, a star basketball player here at Canaby High School, and a member of the Student Council. Wayne is a straight-A student, a star baseball player, a tennis player here at Canaby High School, a writer for the school newspaper, a member of the school choir, a member of the Drama club, and a member of the Student Council. Trina is the daughter of Mr. and Mrs. William Sands, and Wayne is the son of Mr. Richard McGuire and Mrs. Beverly Chancellor."

Just then Kerry and her escort walked into the gym.

"This is Senior maid Kerry Branson," said the assistant principal, "and her escort, Casey Mack."

Kerry and her escort waved, and everyone applauded.

"Kerry is a straight-A student," said the assistant principal, "a member of the school choir, Drama club, and Youth America Campus Club. Casey is a straight-A student, he plays football, baseball, and tennis, he's the Senior Class President, a member of the Future Business Leaders of America, and a member of the Vocational and Industrial Clubs of America. Kerry is the granddaughter of Mr. Timothy Woodall and Mrs. Eudora Pilgrim, and the daughter of the late Mr. Eugene Woodall and the late Ms. Jennifer Branson. Casey is the son of Mr. Alex Buckalew and Mrs. Rebecca Mack."

Meanwhile, Keisha and David were still standing outside the gym, waiting to be introduced.

"Well, are you ready, David?" asked Keisha.

"Yes, Keisha," said David. "I'm ready for anything."

Just then Keisha and David prepared to be introduced. When they did go inside the gym, the entire crowd applauded for them. Keisha had the queen's crown on.

"This is our 1995 Homecoming Queen, Keisha Blackledge," said the assistant principal, "and her escort, David Malone."

Just then Keisha and David waved to everyone.

"Keisha is a varsity football cheerleader, a member of the Future Business Leaders of America, and president of the Student Council. David is a member of the Drug Education Council, and a member of Students Against Drunk Drivers. They are both straight-A students, members of the school choir, members of the Drama club, part of the school newspaper, members of the National Honor Society, and were voted Senior Class Favorites. They are also members of the Distributive Education Clubs of America and the Youth America Campus Club. Keisha is the daughter of Ms. Hilda Blackledge, and David is the son of Mr. and Mrs. Joey Malone."

"So now all of you know about this year's homecoming court," said the principal.

Around three-twenty that afternoon, the main street of downtown Canaby was lined with people that were about to see the high school homecoming parade. Some merchants of downtown Canaby were closed as a direct result of the parade, and the doors of the Canaby City Hall were locked. Soon, the parade started and two drum majorettes were carrying a sign saying, "Canaby High School Homecoming." The band followed, playing their homecoming song. After the band, the football and basketball cheerleaders marched and cheered in the parade. Then the spectators saw the floats of several school clubs, including the National Honor Society, the Future Business Leaders of America, the Distributive Education Clubs of America, the Vocational and Industrial Clubs of America, the French club, the Spanish club, the Debate Committee, the school newspaper staff, the school choir and Drama club, the Drug Education Council, Students Against Drunk Drivers, the Student Council, the Youth America Campus Club, and the Fellowship of Christian Athletes, in the parade. Candy was being thrown out into the streets.

After the school club floats, the parade spectators saw the Dream Daisies dance team members marching in the parade. Then the spectators saw the homecoming float, which had the five homecoming maids and their escorts. The maids and their escorts waved to the crowd, and they waved back. They even threw candy to some spectators. Finally the spectators saw the float that was carrying Keisha and David. This was the float for the queen and her escort. Keisha and David were both waving to the crowd, as well as throwing candy into the streets.

"Are you having fun, David?" asked Keisha.

"Yes," said David. "I haven't done this in a long time."

"I know how you feel, David," said Keisha.

Soon after, the parade spectators started clearing the streets.

Around seven-thirty that night at Warrior Stadium, the football game was about to begin, and the place was packed. There were over five thousand football fans that were seeing the homecoming game, which was a Region 3-5A showdown between Canaby and Lauderdale Creek. Both teams were first and second in the standings, and were playing for the Region 3-5A football championship crown. But while Lauderdale Creek was in first place, undefeated; and Canaby was in second place, with a record of seven and one, Canaby was seen as a huge favorite. Both teams, five and zero in Region 3-5A, had already clinched Class 5A playoff berths, and were ranked in the Mississippi High School Activities Association Top 20 football poll. Lauderdale Creek was no. 3 and Canaby was no. 9. Lauderdale Creek was also ranked no. 1 in the Jackson Clarion-Ledger Super 10 poll.

When the game did start, the cheerleaders cheered, the football players for both teams ran through the appropriate posters, and the bands were playing. The huge crowd was applauding. After a while, the Canaby team kicked the ball off to the Lauderdale Creek team. A running back for the visiting team caught the ball, and made it all the way to the 35-yard line before being tackled. While both teams were playing really hard, lots of press members were at the game. The cheerleaders for both teams were cheering, and the fans on the home side were rooting for Canaby, while the fans on the visiting side were rooting for Lauderdale Creek.

Meanwhile, the lines to both concession stands were long. A number of football fans were buying refreshments. However, Latasha, who had just bought a soda, was standing at the top of the student section. Like a lot of other students, she was cheering for the Canaby team. The dance team members, in their usual place above the band in the stands, were also cheering for the Canaby team. But when Lauderdale Creek scored the first touchdown, the fans that were cheering Canaby on became shocked. The Canaby cheerleaders began cheering, only for Lauderdale Creek to make the extra point with a successful two-point conversion. The score was eight to zero in favor of Lauderdale Creek with six-thirty-eight to go in the first quarter.

The homecoming maids and escorts were seated at the right end of the field, waiting for the homecoming ceremonies.

"Are you okay, David?" asked Keisha.

"Yes," said David. "I'm fine. I'm just ready to get this thing over with."

"We know how you feel, David," said Kerry.

"Are you staying for the homecoming dance?" asked the Freshman maid.

"Yes, I'm staying for the homecoming dance," said David.

Later that night, Canaby was leading Lauderdale Creek by a score of fifteen to eight in the second quarter when it was second down at the Canaby 42. Lauderdale Creek had possession of the ball. The quarterback threw the ball to a running back that ran all the way to the 19 before being thrown to the ground. But on the next play, the running back that got the ball ran all the way into the end zone to score a touchdown. The score was then fifteen to fourteen in Canaby's favor.

Soon, it was halftime at Warrior Stadium. Lauderdale Creek was leading Canaby by a score of twenty-seven to fifteen. During the half-time show, the band played, the dance team performed, and everyone in the stands was enjoying the halftime show. When it was time to crown Keisha, the homecoming maids and their escorts were standing out on the field. Keisha and David were also standing together.

"At this time we would like to crown our 1995 Homecoming Queen, Keisha Blackledge," said the announcer. "On the field with this year's homecoming court are our ring bearer for this year, Charisse McIntire, the daughter of Mr. and Mrs. Mark McIntire, and this year's crown bearer, Corsiana Bernhard, the daughter of Mr. and Mrs. Walter Bernhard."

At that moment the ring bearer placed the lady's ring on the middle finger of Keisha's right hand, and the men's ring on the middle finger of David's right hand. Then the crown bearer handed the crown to the homecoming queen from the previous year, and she placed the crown on Keisha's head. At that moment everyone in the stadium began to applaud for Keisha and David.

"Congratulations to our 1995 Homecoming Queen," said the announcer, "Keisha Blackledge, and her escort, David Malone."

A while later, Keisha was being interviewed by members of the press, and the area around the concession stand was crowded. Meanwhile, Courtney and the other 35 dance team members were talking to David and congratulating him.

"You did excellent out on the field, David," said Courtney. "If I had been a part of the homecoming court, you would have been my escort."

"Thank you, Courtney," said David.

"If I had been on the homecoming court, he would have been my escort," said another dance team member.

"Maybe one of us can choose him for an escort in college," said another dance team member. "Don't you all think so?"

"Maybe so," said a third dance team member. "Maybe Courtney can if she and David go to the same college next year."

"That's right," said Courtney. "You're going to Canaby Junior College in the fall, David," said Courtney, "aren't you?"

"Possibly," said David. "This is really sweet of you all, thinking of me for a future escort, but I don't think Keisha would be too happy about it."

"When the time comes for me to be part of the homecoming court," said Courtney, "I'll still choose you."

"That's very sweet of you," said Courtney.

"Why don't we take pictures of David?" suggested a fourth dance team member. "I have my camera with me."

"That's an excellent idea," said a fifth dance team member.

While the third quarter of the football game was underway—and both teams were playing really hard, the dance team members were taking several pictures. Each picture that was taken involved David and at least one dance team member. Some involved David and several dance team members. For one picture, two dance team members posed on either side of David, and for another picture, a thirteen-year-old girl took a picture of all the dance team members posing with David.

Later in the game, David was at the concession stand buying a soda when Kerry found him.

"David, you did excellent in the halftime show," she said.

"Thank you, Kerry," said David.

"He did really excellent," said a dance team member. "We're taking good care of him."

"What do you mean you all are taking good care of him?" asked Kerry.

"Me, Courtney, and the other dance team members are watching him until Keisha gets back," said the dance team member.

"Oh," thought Kerry. "Well, just don't make him nervous."

Meanwhile, Keisha was back in the football stadium. She was looking for David when Latasha and Cheryl spotted her.

"Hey Keisha?" asked Latasha, "you did great in the halftime show."

"Well, thank you," said Keisha.

"You made a really excellent homecoming queen," said Cheryl.

"I knew I was going to," said Keisha, "and I did."

Just then David found Keisha.

"Keisha, I was looking for you earlier," said David.

"Were you?" asked Keisha. "Well, I had to go and speak to the press. But you can talk to me now."

"Well, okay," said David.

Toward the end of the game, Canaby was leading Lauderdale Creek by a score of thirty-five to twenty seven. But Lauderdale Creek had the ball at their 40. It was two forty-eight to go in the fourth quarter. As the cheerleaders for Lauderdale Creek cheered the quarterback got the ball and threw it, but it was intercepted by Canaby. The cheerleaders for Canaby began cheering.

"I'm really happy for the football team," said Keisha. "Aren't you happy for them, David?"

"Yes, Keisha," said David. "I'm really happy for them."

A while later, the score was forty-three to twenty-seven, in favor of Canaby. The clock was running down, and the Canaby quarterback threw the ball to a running back, who scored a touchdown. Canaby won forty-nine to twenty-seven. Everyone on the home side of the stadium was applauding, the football players and cheerleaders were thrilled, and Keisha and David gave each other a big hug.

Later that night, at the Canaby High School homecoming dance, lots of students were slow-dancing to a special song that was playing to honor Keisha and David. Sure enough, Keisha and David were dancing to the song, sharing a conversation at the same time.

"I really enjoyed wearing the queen's crown tonight," said Keisha. "And I really enjoyed escorting you," said David. "Did you know that was my very first time escorting someone in a homecoming ceremony?" "No, I didn't know that," said Keisha. "But I'm glad that you enjoyed being my escort." "Thank you, Keisha," said David. "Can I ask you something?" asked Keisha. "Yes, Keisha," said David.

"After what we experienced tonight," said Keisha, "can you look me in the eyes and say that we really and truly deserve each other?" "Yes, Keisha," said David. "That's just what I wanted to hear," said Keisha.

Keisha and David then kissed each other, in front of everyone at the dance. Would Keisha be able to make a run for prom queen that Spring? Only the following six months stood between Keisha and the priviledge of prom queen.

THREE

Throughout the rest of the fall semester at Canaby High School, most of the student body saw Keisha and David as wonderful role models for the Freshman and Sophomore classes. One afternoon in October, after school, the front of the campus was crowded as thousands of students, most of them freshmen, sophomores, and juniors, were watching as Keisha and David were sitting under a tree sharing a conversation. All of the students that were watching were happy for Keisha and David setting an excellent example with their love for each other.

"David, aren't you glad that we're together?" asked Keisha.

"Yes," said David. "And I can see that lots of other students are happy for the two of us."

"David, mostly the entire student body is happy for us," said Keisha. "I'll bet that when the annual comes out, our picture of Homecoming Queen and escort is going to grace the entire yearbook."

"You know, Keisha," said David, "I'm glad you brought that up. Because I just can't wait for the yearbooks to come out."

"Me, either," said Keisha.

Just then Latasha, Cheryl, and Ronnie arrived outside the school campus when they saw lots of students witnessing Keisha and David as they were kissing.

"Isn't that sweet?" asked Cheryl.

"It is," said Ronnie. "I have a feeling they're going to marry each other one day."

"I wonder if she'll invite us to their wedding," said Latasha.

"She probably will," said Cheryl. "She and David just might invite the entire Senior class to their wedding when it takes place."

Later that night, at Keisha's house in Canaby, Keisha and David were enjoying a pizza and grape sodas while watching a VCR movie.

"Are you okay, David?" asked Keisha.

"Yes, Keisha," said David. "I'm just trying to think about what the future could hold for us."

"I've got a pretty good idea about what the future could hold for the two of us," said Keisha. "Like graduation, prom, the SAT and ACT, college, and maybe the National Merit Finals."

"Can I ask you something?" asked David.

"Sure," said Keisha.

"Do you think I should go to college outside Mississippi?" asked David.

"Well, do you really want to go to college in another state?" asked Keisha.

"I haven't really decided yet," said David. "Besides, I was planning on waiting until close to graduation time and then making my decision."

"That's a good idea," said Keisha. "Why don't we talk to the guidance counselor about it tomorrow?"

"Well, okay," said David.

"Let's enjoy the movie for now," said Keisha, "okay?"

"Okay, Keisha," said David.

Keisha and David started holding hands as they continued to watch the movie.

The next day at school, Keisha, in her cheerleader uniform, and David were sitting at a table in the guidance office looking at college pamphlets. Keisha and David were scheduled to take class favorite pictures later that day.

"David, can I ask you something?" asked Keisha.

"Of course you can, Keisha," said David.

"Do you think we should go to the same college?" asked Keisha.

"I don't know, Keisha," said David. "Why?"

"I mean, we'll be together," said Keisha, "and we can have classes together. Wouldn't that be great?"

"Yes, it would," said David, "but I want it to be the best choice for me."

Just then a counselor arrived on the scene.

"Okay," she said, "you two can come on into my office now."

A while later, Keisha and David were sitting in the office when the counselor walked in and closed the door.

"I am really proud of both of you for what you all have accomplished here at Canaby High School," said the counselor. "You two are straight-A students, in several school clubs and organizations, and Homecoming Queen and escort."

"Thank you," said Keisha. "Did you know that we're working on Prom Queen and Prom King?"

"We didn't know that," said the counselor. "But good luck though."

"Thank you," said David. "Thank you very much."

"Anyway, have you all taken the Scholastic Aptitude Test or the American College Test yet?" asked the counselor.

"Not yet," said David. "But we plan to within the next month or two."

"But other than the SAT and ACT scores, you all just about have what it takes to get into college," said the counselor. "And one of you, or maybe even both of you, might end up as National Merit Finalists."

"Yeah, maybe," said Keisha. "But we really want to graduate from high school."

When morning break came that day, the halls were noisy and crowded. Some students were at their lockers, others were in the hallways sharing conversations. At the snack bar, which was crowded, Keisha and David were enjoying their morning break favorite: jelly doughnuts and sodas.

"David, you don't have to go to the same college as me if you don't want to," said Keisha.

"I didn't say that," said David. "All I said was that I just want my college decision to be the best choice for me. But when the time comes, I'll call you, and write you, and visit you."

"That's very sweet of you," said Keisha.

Just then Kerry and her best friend, Jenny, arrived at the snack bar.

"Hi, David," said Kerry.

"Hey, Jenny and Kerry," said David.

"Are you all ready to take the Class Favorite pictures?" asked Jenny.

"Of course we are," said Keisha. "We're also excited about it. That's why I've got my cheerleader uniform on."

When the time came to take the class favorite pictures, Keisha and David, along with six other students that were voted class favorites, were outside the school waiting to take the pictures. When the photographer arrived, he talked to Keisha, David, and the other students before he took the pictures. First, he took the Freshman Class Favorite picture. Then he took the Sophomore Class Favorite picture. Then he took the Junior Class Favorite picture. Finally, he took the picture of Keisha and David. This was the Senior Class Favorite picture. In posing for the picture, Keisha and David were under a tree on the school campus. Keisha was standing beside David, who was sitting on a bench under the tree.

Around three p.m. that afternoon, in the school library, David was doing homework when Keisha, who was still wearing her cheerleader uniform, walked in to see about him.

"Are you okay, David?" asked Keisha.

"Yes, Keisha," said David. "I'm fine. I'm just doing some homework."

"Well, I was just wondering if you could come and watch me cheer this afternoon," said Keisha.

"If I get a chance, I will," said David. "But good luck, though."

"Thanks, David," said Keisha. "Cheerleader practice doesn't start until about four o' clock today."

"Wait a minute," said David, "you all have got cheerleader practice today?"

"That's right," said Keisha.

"You didn't tell me that this morning," said David.

"Well, I should have," said Keisha.

"It's okay, Keisha," said David. "I just didn't know that you and the other cheerleaders were practicing. But I kind of know why you didn't tell me."

"Listen, David," said Keisha, "if I'm distracting you from your homework. . ."

"Oh, no, Keisha," said David. "Not at all."

"Well, okay," said Keisha. "I just don't want to keep you from doing your homework."

"I tell you what, Keisha," said David. "As soon as I get a break, I'll come and watch you all practice."

"Well, okay," said Keisha.

"But good luck, though," said David.

"Thank you, David," said Keisha. "Thank you very much."

Keisha and David then kissed each other.

"I'll see you later," said Keisha. "Bye."

"Bye, Keisha," said David.

Keisha then left the library, and David then continued to do his homework.

Later that afternoon, during cheerleader practice on the football field, Keisha and the other football cheerleaders, all wearing their uniforms, were working on some of their cheers while the basketball cheerleaders, who were also wearing their uniforms, were in the football bleachers watching.

After a while, David, coming from the library, arrived on the football field to watch his girlfriend practice her cheers. A while after David sat down in the bleachers, the basketball cheerleaders walked up to him.

"Hey, David," said one cheerleader.

"Oh, hi," said David.

"Did you come to watch your girlfriend cheer?" asked another cheerleader.

"Yes, I did," said David. "Why?"

"Because she's an excellent cheerleader out there," said a third cheerleader.

"Well, thanks for being so curious," said David, "because she really means a lot to me."

"We mean a lot to you, too," said a fourth cheerleader.

"I beg your pardon," said David.

"We mean a lot to you, too," said the fourth cheerleader.

"Well, okay," said David.

Throughout the cheerleader practice, David and the basketball cheerleaders watched as Keisha and the other football cheerleaders practiced their cheers like crazy. While practicing, Keisha was proving to David that she was a very special girl, even while cheering on the football field.

About an hour later, as it was getting close to sunset, Keisha and the rest of the football cheerleaders were finished practicing. David and the basketball cheerleaders then went onto the field.

"Keisha, you did excellent on the football field," said David.

"Thank you, David," said Keisha. "Thank you for coming out here to see me cheer."

"It's no problem, Keisha," said David.

"He'd do anything for you, Keisha," said a basketball cheerleader.

"Isn't that sweet of him?" asked a football cheerleader.

"It is," said another basketball cheerleader. "It's very, very sweet of him."

"Listen, girls," said David, "I took a break from my homework to come out here and see her."

"That's still very sweet of you, David," said Keisha.

"Wouldn't it be great if they married each other before the end of the school term?" asked a football cheerleader.

"That's a great idea," said a basketball cheerleader. "Maybe they should get married by the end of the school year."

"Oh, I don't think David and I are ready to settle down yet," said Keisha. "But if and when the time comes for us to get married, we'll invite you all to the wedding."

"Well, we're really looking forward to it," said a basketball cheerleader.

"Hey David?" asked Keisha, "wanna go for a ride?"

"That will be great, Keisha," said David.

Just then the football and basketball cheerleaders looked on and smiled as Keisha and David walked out of the football field together.

"Don't they make a cute couple?" asked a basketball cheerleader.

"Yes, Savannah," said a football cheerleader. "They make a very cute couple."

Around sunset that evening, as the sun was about to go down, Keisha, who was still wearing her cheerleader uniform, and David were standing on a hilltop outside of Canton in the Jackson area. They were sharing a conversation while getting ready to see a sunset.

"Keisha, you have really made this day special for me," said David.

"It's no problem, David," said Keisha. "Besides, I just wanted our class favorite picture day to be more special."

"At least now we can get ready for our big run for college and graduation," said David.

"But what about test day?" asked Keisha, "and yearbook time, and prom night?"

"We can't forget about those events," said David.

"David, I'm hoping that prom night will be very special this year," said Keisha.

"I'm sure it will be," said David.

"But it would be more special if I was the prom queen," said Keisha, "and you were the prom king."

"Really?" asked David.

"Yes," said Keisha. "Do you think I'm beautiful enough?"

"Of course I do, Keisha," said David. "If you want to be the prom queen, then I have no problem with it."

"But what I'm really hoping for is you and me having the most wonderful Senior year of high school," said Keisha, "in addition to graduating from high school with highest honors."

"I feel the same way, too," said David.

"I'm glad you do," said Keisha. "Can I ask you something?"

"You sure can," said David.

"After what happened to us at school today," said Keisha, "including all the cheerleaders seeing us as a very special couple, can you look me in the eyes and say that we really and truly deserve each other?"

"Yes, I can, Keisha," said David.

"That's just what I wanted to hear," said Keisha.

Keisha and David then kissed each other, as the sun was going down. While kissing, Keisha lightly touched David's cheek and jaw, and even raised her left foot up. As the sun began sinking, Keisha was still kissing David.

Around midnight that night, as Keisha and David were both fast asleep in bed, the moon in the sky was shining brightly, and the night lights in downtown Jackson, as well as metro Jackson and the entire surrounding area, looked very bright and beautiful.

About a month later at Canaby High School, the annual school beauty pageant took place. The auditorium was packed as over five-thousand spectators were watching the pageant. Keisha was one of twenty-eight beauties, while David was one of eleven beaus competing in the pageant.

While Cheryl and Ronnie were emceeing the pageant, Keisha and nine of the other twenty-eight beauties competed in swimsuit, talent, question / interview, and congeniality competitions. The eleven beaus were narrowed down to five, and David and the other four competed in talent and congeniality competitions. Everyone watching the pageant cheered for Keisha and David.

Toward the end of the pageant, the ten beauties were narrowed down to five, and the five beaus went on stage. Keisha and the other four beauties were on the left of the stage, and David and the other four beaus were on the right of the stage. The judges of the pageant had their results in. Keisha was crowned most beautiful and David was crowned favorite beau. The other four beauties were all given flowers. Everyone applauded as Keisha and David walked the aisle as most beautiful and favorite beau.

After the pageant, the outside of the school was crowded as lots of reporters and members of the Jackson Clarion-Ledger, as well as members of the school newspaper, were doing stories on the pageant, as well as taking pictures of Keisha, David, and the other eight winners of the school beauty pageant. News reporters of the three Jackson TV stations were also at the school to report on the pageant.

That night, at a restaurant in north Jackson, Keisha and David were having a romantic candlelight dinner. Everyone at the restaurant was all dressed up, but most of the employees and patrons were dressed in after-five attire. There was a special jazz band, consisting of a pianist, drum player, bass player, keyboard player, and tenor saxophonist, playing a slow song at the restaurant.

"David, wouldn't it be wonderful if we did get to be prom queen and prom king this spring?" asked Keisha.

"Yes, Keisha," said David. "It would be really, really wonderful."

"And I'll be this beautiful girl with a dark and lonely childhood past and emotional scars," said Keisha.

"That's right, Keisha," said David. "I'll bet the entire school will be proud of you if you ran for prom queen."

"And wouldn't it be great if you ended up being the prom king?" asked Keisha.

"Oh, I don't know about that," said David.

Just then a waitress went to Keisha and David's table.

"Is everything okay over here?" asked the waitress.

"Yes," said Keisha. "We're wonderful."

"Well, okay," said the waitress. "Call me if you all need anything."

"We will," said David.

The waitress then left the table, and Keisha and David carried on with their conversation. Soon, the saxophone player began playing in the song, and lots of patrons began slow-dancing to the song.

"Would you like to dance, David?" asked Keisha.

"I'd love to, Keisha," said David.

Just then Keisha and David started slow-dancing to the song. She put her arms around him. Lots of employees at the restaurant were thrilled to see Keisha and David slow-dancing along with most of the other patrons at the restaurant.

"Isn't that sweet?" asked a waitress.

"It is," said a waiter. "It's very, very sweet."

The next day at school, the snack bar, as well as the hallways, were noisy and crowded. It was during morning break, and Keisha, David, and Latasha were all talking about the Senior year while enjoying snacks.

"Keisha, you and David are such an inspiration to everyone here at Canaby High School," said Latasha.

"Well, we just want our Senior year to be special," said Keisha.

"See, this is the one moment that we thought would never come in our lives," said David.

"Listen, I know that you and David were abused and beaten as children," said Latasha, "and that the odds of you two succeeding in life were little back then. But you all are having the best high school Senior year there is. Isn't that something to be proud of?"

"Yes, Latasha," said David. "There's a lot of students here at Canaby High School that have faith in us."

"David, the football and basketball cheerleaders have faith in us, too," said Keisha.

"Oh, I forgot about that day," said David.

Just then Cheryl, Ronnie, and several of Latasha's friends arrived at the snack bar.

"Hey, Keisha," said Cheryl.

"Congratulations in the beauty pageant," said Ronnie.

"Thank you, Ronnie," said David.

"Cheryl? Ronnie?" asked Latasha, "They are an inspiration to the entire student body here at Canaby High School."

"That's right, Latasha," said Cheryl. "They're straight-A students, Keisha's president of the Student Council, and David's the lead member of Students Against Drunk Drivers."

"And they're in lots of other school clubs," said Ronnie, " like the choir and Drama club and the Youth America Campus Club."

"But we still have to take the ACT and SAT tests," said Keisha.

"We plan to before this semester is over," said David.

Throughout the rest of the semester, Keisha and David used their classes to get ready to take the standardized tests. They took part in class, and studied at home even harder in their spare time. But as president of the Student Council, Keisha continued doing her duty at the student council meetings. And David continued going to the SADD and Drug Ed meetings and continued performing his duties. And during school breaks, they continued their rounds of socializing, as more and more students, especially those among the Senior class, became more and more happy for them.

When the day of the SAT test came, Keisha, in her car, drove to the SAT testing center, which was located in north Jackson near the Northpark Mall, and David, in his car, followed her. They took Interstate 20 West, passing by such exits as Airport Road / Hwy. 475, which led to the Jackson International Airport, Hwy. 468, which went to Flowood, and U.S. Hwy. 49, which went to Oakwood City, Magee, Hattiesburg, and the Mississippi Gulf Coast. Then they took Interstate 55 North, passing by such exits as Pearl Street, which led to downtown Jackson, High Street, which led to the State Capitol and lots of government offices, Fortification Street, Woodrow Wilson Avenue, Lakeland Drive, and Briarwood Drive.

Traffic on I-55 in north Jackson was very heavy, and Keisha and David were passing several stores, restaurants, and hotels. When they got to the County Line Road exit, they got off of the interstate, and headed to the SAT center. They passed the Northpark Mall, as well as more restaurants and stores. Soon, they were at the SAT center, and it was around two p.m. in the afternoon.

When the test started, Keisha, David, and forty-six other high school students started reading the tests and filling in answers as the test proctor was watching. Some of the students were under a lot of pressure, but Keisha and David were very confident that they would do good on the test. The test was supposed to last for two-and-a-half hours.

When breaktime came, halfway through the test, Keisha and David, as well as a few other students, were enjoying sodas in the refreshment room. Keisha and David were feeling good about the first half of the test, and they didn't expect the second half of the test to be any different.

Later that night, at David's house in Canaby, David was fast asleep in bed when his mother and father both walked into his room to check up on him. His mother turned his lamp on, and he woke up.

"Are you okay, David?" asked his father.

"Yes, Dad," said David. "I'm okay."

"How did you do on the test today?" asked his mother.

"I think I did okay on it," said David.

"You know, David," said his dad, "we're really, very proud of you."

"You're a straight-A student," said his mother, "you're in several school clubs, and you got to escort the homecoming queen for this year."

"Hey, that was my own girlfriend," said David.

"But think about the bright side, David," said his mother. "She's very popular at Canaby High School. And we're proud of her for choosing you as her boyfriend."

"She and David have something tragic in common," said his father. "We had to adopt David back in 1992 after he ended up in one foster home after another, remember?"

"I know where this is going," said his mother. "Keisha's mom did adopt her after a string of group homes. But she and our son actually have something in common."

"That's right," said his father. "She and David are going to be graduating from Canaby High School in May with highest honors. And I'm very proud of him."

"I'm proud of you, too," said his mother.

"Thank you," said David. "Thank you very much."

At that moment David gave his father a big hug, and then he gave his mother a big hug.

Meanwhile, at Keisha's house, Keisha was also fast asleep in bed. Soon, her mother walked into her room, wanting to talk to her. Keisha turned her lamp on, and woke up.

"Hey Keisha?" she asked, "are you okay?"

"Yes, mom," said Keisha. "I'm okay."

"How did you do on your test today?" asked David.

"I probably did okay," said Keisha.

"So, that's good to hear," said her mother. "You know, Keisha, I'm so proud of you."

"Thank you, mom," said Keisha. "I wonder if David's doing okay?"

"I'm sure he is," said her mother. "I'm proud of him for giving you his time."

"We have something in common," said Keisha, "but thanks. I'll talk to him about it at school Monday."

"When the time comes for you and David to graduate," said her mother, "I'll be there to watch you all walk across the field and get your diplomas."

"Thank you, mom," said Keisha. "Thank you very much."

At that moment Keisha gave her mother a big hug.

"I'm very proud of you, Keisha," said her mother.

"Thank you, mom," said Keisha.

When it came time for Keisha and David to take the ACT test, they headed to the ACT testing center. They took Intrestate 20 West, but this time, they were headed to west Jackson, where the ACT testing center was located. They passed such exits as State Street, Gallatin Street, Terry Road, Ellis Avenue, and Loop 220, as well as several car dealerships, hotels, restaurants and even a shopping center. Traffic on Interstate 20 was very heavy. Soon, they were at the test center, which was located on Robinson Road just before U.S. Highway 80 in west Jackson, near the Metrocenter Mall.

The ACT testing room was crowded that Saturday, as Keisha and David were among a lot of high school students taking the test. At five p.m., the test started and Keisha, David, and the other sixty-one students began reading the questions and selecting answers. The proctor watched the students carefully. Again, some of the students were under pressure, but Keisha and David were still confident that they would do good on the test.

One afternoon in December, in the guidance office at school, Keisha and David were waiting to find out their test scores. While Keisha was standing and David was seated on a couch, they were both very, very happy. It was around three p.m., and school was over for that day.

"Are you okay, David?" asked Keisha.

"Yes, Keisha," said David. "I am okay."

"I thought about you the rest of the weekend," said Keisha.

"Did you?" asked David. "That's so sweet of you."

"Can I ask you something, David?" asked Keisha.

"Sure you can, Keisha," said David.

"If we did happen to go to the same college together next fall," said Keisha, "do you think we could have some classes together?"

"Maybe so, Keisha," said David.

Just then a guidance counselor walked out into the hallway.

"Hey Keisha? David?" asked the counselor, "great news."

"What is it?" asked Keisha.

"The SAT and ACT test scores are back in," said the counselor. "Keisha, 960 on the SAT, 22 composite on the ACT. David, 850 on the SAT, 19 composite on the ACT."

At that moment, Keisha and David gave each other a big hug.

Outside the campus, the entire student body, including the Senior class, was lined up waiting on the outcome of the SAT and ACT. Just then Keisha and David walked out of the school.

"I've got wonderful news," said Keisha. "David and I both passed the SAT and ACT tests."

At that moment all of the students that were standing outside the campus applauded for Keisha and David. With the SAT and ACT tests out of the way, Keisha and David could then start looking forward to the rest of the Senior year, as well as their college futures.

FOUR

Three months later, as prom season was approaching, Keisha began to think about being the prom queen of her senior class, since the entire school saw her as an excellent homecoming queen. There was plenty of time for Keisha to prepare for prom night, but since Keisha was trying to build more memories from her Senior year, she thought that being prom queen would add to that list.

It was around seven o' clock on a Monday evening in early March, and Keisha had taken a ride to a park in metro Jackson. She was having a very depressing day, and she was worried about being the prom queen of her class at Canaby High School. She wanted to add prom queen to her list of achievements, knowing it would make her Senior year more special. She wanted her Senior year to be very, very special, mainly because she has an abusive past, as well as emotional scars. After a while David showed up at the park. He had been concerned about her all day.

"Hey Keisha?" asked David, "are you okay?"

Keisha then noticed David at the park.

"David, how did you manage to find me down here?" asked Keisha.

"I've been worried about you all day," said David.

"David, I said I needed some time alone," said Keisha. "I was hoping you would respect that."

"Keisha, I know you're going through tough times right now," said David, "but I promise you that it's going to be much, much better for you in a few days."

"The elections for prom queen are next week," said Keisha, "and I want to add prom queen to my list of honors."

"Maybe you can," said David. "You just have to follow your heart."

"Maybe you're right," said Keisha. "I shouldn't let my dark childhood keep me from being a success."

"Besides, take a look at how popular you are at Canaby High School," said David. "You're on the principal's list, you're the lead singer of the school choir, you're the star varsity football cheerleader, and you're even hot stuff in beauty pageants."

"You do have a point there," said Keisha. "I shouldn't throw away my popularity over child abuse and emotional scars. Thanks for telling me this."

"That's no problem," said David. "Anytime you need me, I'll be there for you. Okay?"

"That's really, very sweet of you, David," said Keisha.

Keisha and David then hugged each other.

"I guess following my heart is a good idea," said Keisha.

Around sunset that evening, David drove Keisha home. They rode through downtown Jackson, and even rode by the State Capitol building, as well as the Governor's Mansion.

"You know, this prom queen honor, if I get it, is really going to mean a lot to me," said Keisha.

"And it'll mean something to me, too," said David. "But just follow your heart, and there's a good chance that it will come true."

"But, even if I do get to be prom queen, I'm going to be really, really embarrassed if someone was to laugh at me," said Keisha.

"Keisha, nobody is going to laugh at you," said David.

"But what if it happens?" asked Keisha.

"It's not going to happen," said David. "Trust me."

"How can you be sure?" asked Keisha.

"Keisha, if you do get to be prom queen," said David, "I am going to take every precaution necessary to see to it that you do not get embarrassed in any way."

"Do you promise?" asked Keisha.

"I promise," said David.

"Well, okay," said Keisha. "That's very sweet of you."

On their way back to Canaby, Keisha and David stopped at a

convenience store near the Mississippi Coliseum in Jackson. David then parked the car in the store's parking lot.

"Keisha, I'll be right back," said David.

"Okay," said Keisha. "I'll just wait right here."

David then went inside the store, leaving Keisha alone in the car. While David was inside the store, Keisha was looking outside the window of the car, thinking about what it would be like to be elected as the prom queen of her class. Suddenly a white BMW blasting with loud music pulled up to gas tank no. 7 at the store. The six girls that met David at the carnival then jumped out of the car. When they spotted Keisha, they began talking about her.

"Isn't that Keisha Blackledge?" asked the driver of the BMW.

"Yeah," said a girl in the group. "I heard she was gonna be the prom queen."

"She's not gonna be the prom queen," said the driver of the BMW. "She could never be a prom queen."

"You don't know that," said another girl in the group.

"Yes, I do," said the driver. "She's been in and out of foster homes, she's into drugs and alcohol, she's been beaten, raped, and abused as a child, and she's been to jail."

"Any girl can be a prom queen," said a third girl.

"Any girl except Keisha," said the driver.

"But think about it," said a fourth girl. "Keisha could surprise all of us."

"I'm telling all of you," said the driver, "there's no way that Keisha could possibly be a prom queen."

Suddenly Keisha, filled with anger and frustration, jumped out of the car, and started running away from the girls as fast as she could. The girls then started laughing at her. Just then David came out of the store with two blue cream sodas, one for him, and one for Keisha. He noticed the six girls laughing and ignored them. But when he got to the car, he realized Keisha was gone. The girls started laughing at him. He was really, really angry.

"Hey, where's Keisha?" asked David, in a state of anger.

"How should we know?" asked the driver of the BMW. "We don't keep up with Keisha."

"I don't see anything funny here," said David. "Where is Keisha?"

"I think she went down the highway," said a fifth girl.

David went to his car when he suddenly turned around. "Did you know I could have all of you put in jail for this?" asked David.

"You're funny, David," said a sixth girl. "You're really funny."

"You all really think so," said David. "We'll see who gets the last laugh."

Just then David left the premises of the convenience store, and the six girls kept laughing and giggling.

"He is really silly," said the second girl, whose name was Leandra Pitts.

David drove around in hopes of finding Keisha. He crossed a bridge that led from the coliseum back to downtown Jackson. He stopped on the bridge and looked around, but saw no sign of Keisha. He then went down nearly every street in the downtown area, but he still couldn't find Keisha.

"Where could Keisha be?" David asked himself.

Meanwhile, Keisha was sitting under the bridge that led to downtown, crying. She was upset because the six problem girls teased her and upset her. Just then a motorist spotted Keisha, and stopped to offer her a ride.

"Hey, do you need a ride?" he asked.

"Yes," said Keisha. "I'm trying to find my boyfriend."

"Well, come on," said the motorist.

Just then the motorist and Keisha left the scene, and started looking for David.

David, however, was still riding around in an attempt to locate Keisha. He drove around the Jackson Zoo, the old Jackson Mall, and near Mississippi Veterans Memorial Stadium, but still saw no sign of Keisha.

Keisha and the motorist rode down U.S. Highway 80, going westbound, in an attempt to track David down, but they did not see him. But when they went through the green light at the intersection of

U.S. 80 and Ellis Avenue, they kept straight on U.S. 80 West. The light then changed, and, to a big surprise, David went through the light, keeping straight on South Ellis Avenue and heading toward Interstate 20. It was around eight-fifteen, and the sky was dark.

"Keisha has got to be around here somewhere," said David.

David then took Interstate 20 East. He was still on the lookout for Keisha.

Meanwhile, Keisha and the motorist had stopped at a fast-food restaurant, asking for help in trying to find David.

"This girl here is looking for her boyfriend," said the motorist.

"He has to be around here somewhere," said Keisha.

"Well, maybe I should come with you all," said the woman, who was a waitress at the restaurant.

"We'd really appreciate it if you did," said the motorist.

Meanwhile, David was traveling down Interstate 55 North, and had just passed the High Street exit when the car with Keisha in it entered the interstate. But David, still trying to find Keisha, was not at all aware that the car Keisha was in was behind him. After a while, David gave up.

Meanwhile, in the Canaby High School gymnasium, an MHSAA Class 5A High School Basketball south state playoff game was taking place. Canaby was playing Madison Central with elimination on the line. David arrived in the gym looking for Keisha, but to his surprise, Canaby was up by fifteen points with four-twenty-one to go in the second quarter. Everyone in the stands on the home side of the gym cheered with excitement, while the cheerleaders kept cheering with the crowd. David sat in the stands and watched the game, but after a while Rosalynn, his best friend, spotted him at the game.

"Hello, David," she said. "How are you doing?"

"Rosalynn, I wasn't looking forward to seeing you here," said David. "Better yet, I didn't expect to see you again until this summer."

"Well, I surprised you," said Rosalynn.

"You sure did surprise me," said David, "but I believe you surprised me at a really bad time."

"Why?" asked Rosalynn. "What's wrong?"

"Because earlier this evening, I went to a convenience store in Jackson to . . . ," said David. He was cut off by the six girls that gave him trouble at the convenience store in Jackson. They had just walked into the gym.

"Hey, David," said the ringleader, whose name was Carla Simpson.

"You remember us?"

"I can't believe this," said David.

"You can't believe what?" asked the third girl, whose name was Jennifer Cameron, "the fact that we're in love with you?"

"David, don't let them get to you," said Rosalynn.

"They ran Keisha away," said David, "and now I can't find her anywhere."

"So now you'll have to settle for us," said Carla.

"If I were one of you all, I would cool it," said Rosalynn.

"But David's our favorite guy," said the sixth girl, whose name was Melanie Warren.

"They do this to me every day at school," said David.

Just then several of David's real friends saw what was going on, and intervened immediately.

"David, are those girls bothering you again?" asked Jenny.

"I don't know what they're up to," said David.

"David, it's okay," said Rosalynn.

"I don't think it is," said Jenny. "The last thing he needs is for them to make him lose his cool."

"I know you all are trying to make me feel better," said David, "but I'm . . ."

"So deeply in love with us," said Leandra, cutting David off, "and we don't blame you at all."

"I think you young ladies had better back off," said Jenny.

Meanwhile, a tearful, frustrated Keisha was sitting on the steps to the front door of the main building on the Canaby High School campus. She had just been dropped off at the school to look for David.

"I just hope David isn't mad at me," said Keisha.

Just then she walked into the gymnasium. When she got into

the gym, she realized that she was missing a really good game. But she was mostly concentrated on finding David. When she spotted him in the bleachers, she immediately ran to him and apologized to him for running away from the convenience store.

"David, I'm really sorry for running away from the curb store," said Keisha.

"It's okay, Keisha," said David. "I know you were trying to get away from those silly girls."

"Can I say something to both of you?" asked Rosalynn.

"What's that?" asked Keisha.

"Don't let those silly girls get to you all," said Rosalynn.

"Well, okay," said David.

"They've already made me mad," said Keisha.

"I'm telling you," said Rosalynn. "All they're trying to do is push both of you over the edge."

"Well, they trouble David most of the time," said Keisha.

"Yeah, Keisha," said David, "that's true."

"David, promise me that you won't let those silly girls upset you from this night forward," said Rosalynn.

"Okay," said David, "but I doubt that it'll work."

"I'll see to it that they don't get to him," said Keisha.

"You do that for me," said Rosalynn, "okay, Keisha?"

"Okay, Ros," said Keisha.

Later that night at home, Keisha was in her bedroom looking out her window at the stars and night lights when her mother walked into her room.

"Hey Keisha?" asked her mother.

"Yes?" asked Keisha.

"Can I come in and talk to you for a minute?" asked her mother.

"I suppose so," said Keisha.

Keisha's mother then walked into her room to talk to her.

"Keisha, I know you and David both have physical and emotional scars," said her mother, "and I'm aware that some of the kids at school are making fun of both of you because of it."

"They're doing it more so to David," said Keisha.

"Just don't let them get to you or David," said her mother. "Because all they want to see is either you or David throw a fit in front of everyone."

"Well, thanks for telling me," said Keisha. "I'll talk to David about it at school tomorrow."

"Keisha, if they continue to make fun of you or David," said her mother, "just let me know and I'll take it from there. Okay?"

"Well, okay," said Keisha.

"Good night, Keisha," said her mother.

"Good night, mom," said Keisha.

When Keisha's mom left the room, Keisha turned her light off, and went to bed. While she was asleep, she happened to be thinking about David.

The next morning at school, the halls were noisy, and packed with students. It was during morning break, and David was at his locker when Jenny walked up to him. He was having a very rough day.

"Hey, David," said Jenny.

"Hello, Jenny," said David.

"Are you feeling better?" asked Jenny.

"No," said David.

"Why?" asked Jenny. "What's wrong?"

"Those girls have pestured me all morning long," said David. "It seems like there's nothing I can do to stop them from bothering me."

"It's going to be okay, David," said Jenny. "I promise."

"Well, I hope it works," said David.

"David, why don't you let me walk you to your next class?" suggested Jenny, "okay?"

"Well, okay," said David.

At that moment David closed his locker, and started walking with Jenny. They continued their conversation while the halls were still noisy and crowded.

"David, there's a dance taking place at Canaby Junior High School on the eighteenth," said Jenny, "and I was thinking maybe you'd like to go to that dance."

"I don't see a problem with it," said David.

"Well, maybe I could meet you there," said Jenny.

"But what about Keisha?" asked David.

"I'll talk to Keisha about it," said Jenny, "okay?"

"Well, okay," said David.

Just then David made it to his class.

"I'll save seats for both of you in the cafeteria today," said Jenny.

"Okay," said David. "I really appreciate it."

"Bye, David," said Jenny.

"Goodbye, Jenny," said David.

David then took his seat in the U.S. History class.

"Are you feeling better, David?" asked Courtney.

"Not really," said David.

"I'm sure things are going to get better for you," said Courtney. "Better yet, you'll probably be happy by this afternoon."

"Maybe so," said David, "but thanks."

At lunchtime in the cafeteria, Jenny and her friends were sharing a huge conversation when Keisha and David came over. The cafeteria was very crowded.

"Are you feeling better, David?" asked Jenny.

"Yes," said David. "Much, much better."

"Jenny, I need to talk to you about something that's been on my mind all year," said Keisha.

"What do you need to talk about?" asked Jenny.

"I'm thinking about trying out to be the prom queen of the Senior class," said Keisha.

"Are you?" asked Jenny. "I think you'll make a wonderful prom queen."

"That's just what I wanted to hear," said Keisha, "because I talked to David about it, and he's on my side. He told me that I should follow my heart."

"You know, Keisha," said Kerry, "if you do get to be prom queen, you'll be a very special one."

"That's right," said a student named Michael, "because she has a very dark past."

"I don't feel very comfortable talking about my childhood," said Keisha, "but since David has painful emotional scars as well, I'll tell it to you."

"You know we understand, Keisha," said Jenny, "so don't be afraid."

"See, my real parents in Colorado have a history of drug and alcohol abuse," said Keisha, "and when I was seven, they started beating me, and abusing me, both physically and sexually. The abuse continued for about three years, and at eleven, I was placed in a foster home. At thirteen, I moved down here to Mississippi after the lady that's now my mom adopted me."

"Keisha, that's terrible," said Michael.

"That's so sad," said Kerry.

"But I've got a better life here in Mississippi," said Keisha.

"Can you all excuse me for a minute?" asked David. He then walked out of the cafeteria door.

"Now what was that all about?" asked Michael.

"I don't know," said Jenny, "but I'm not going to let David suffer like this."

"Me, either," said Kerry.

Jenny and Kerry then left the cafeteria looking for David. Most of the students were in distress about what was happening. Soon after, Courtney, in a state of anger, immediately stormed out of the cafeteria looking for David. When faculty members in the cafeteria realized what was going on, they began to get worried. Most of the other students were still upset.

"I believe chaos has erupted among the students," said the principal.

Suddenly everyone in the cafeteria was in a daze, while David was in another part of the school having an emotional breakdown. Most of the students were worried about David.

FIVE

David was at his locker in the hallway when Jenny and Kerry found him.

"David, what's the matter?" asked Jenny.

"It can't be that bad, David," said Kerry.

"I'm just frustrated," said David.

"David, it happened to Keisha, too," said Jenny. "Both of you have the same childhood past. I know this is making you feel bad, but you just have to put it behind you and move on."

"Look, David," said Kerry, "I know you're frustrated about all of this, but it's not your fault that things turned out the way they did. It's not your fault that you've got emotional scars."

Just then Courtney arrived in the hallway.

"I don't like what I'm seeing here," said Courtney. "David, is someone bothering you again?"

"Courtney, David isn't feeling very well," said Jenny.

"The poor guy's dark childhood past is haunting him," said Kerry. "Apparently, Keisha discussed hers in the cafeteria, right in front of him."

"I think David and I need to have a talk," said Courtney.

"You don't know that," said Jenny.

"Yes, I do," said Courtney.

Just then Courtney approached David.

"David, are you okay?" asked Courtney.

"Yes, Courtney," said David, "I'm okay."

"Would you like to go outside and talk to me about this?" asked Courtney.

"Well, okay," said David.

Just then Courtney and David left the hallway.

"I suppose she can comfort him better than we can," said Kerry. Meanwhile, in the office, the assistant principal and secretary were talking when the principal walked in.

"I need to talk to both of you," said the principal.

"Why?" asked the secretary. "What's the matter?"

"Something terrible happened in the cafeteria," said the principal, "and I would like to get to the bottom of it."

"What are you talking about?" asked the assistant principal.

"I don't know what happened," said the principal, "but David Malone walked out of the cafeteria. Then Jenny Phillips and Kerry Branson walked out of the cafeteria. Then, all of a sudden, Courtney Stone stormed out of the cafeteria. Then a lot of other students started hurrying out of the cafeteria."

During afternoon break at the high school, the halls were noisy, and packed with students. But there was also fear in the air. Lots of students in the halls were worried about David. But Jenny and Kerry both knew that he was okay.

"I don't believe this," said Kerry. "Courtney is so desperate to comfort David, and she doesn't even know him very well."

"Maybe she can comfort him better than we can," said Jenny.

"You're probably right," said Kerry. "She probably can give David better advice than we can."

Suddenly the six problem girls walked up to Jenny and Kerry.

"Hey, have you two seen David?" asked Carla.

"Yes, we've seen him," said Jenny.

"Is there something you want with him?" asked Kerry.

"Yes," said the fourth girl, whose name was Latish Benson. "We want to talk to him."

"I don't like where this is going," said Jenny. "You all are the last thing David needs right now."

"You all are out to pick on David," said Kerry. "We know it. You can't fool us about it."

Keisha then walked out of the cafeteria looking for David. She was finished eating lunch. She passed through the noisy, crowded hallway, and when she ran into Jenny and Kerry, she saw the six problem girls.

"Keisha, are you okay?" asked Jenny.

"I'm trying to figure out why they're here," said Keisha.

"We're here because we wanna see David," said Leandra.

"Don't count on it," said Keisha.

"Don't count on what?" asked the fifth girl, whose name was Brittany Warren.

"Don't count on seeing David," said Keisha.

Later that afternoon, Courtney took David to a dairy bar just near Canaby High School for some ice cream, since he was having a rough day. But their ice cream treat was disrupted by the loud, blaring music of the BMW that the six problem girls were in. The problem girls stopped at the dairy bar.

"I really want to thank you for bringing me here and buying me ice cream," said David.

"It's no problem," said Courtney. "Besides, I stop by here after school every day."

"I didn't know that," said David.

"I love buying ice cream after school," said Courtney, as she and David were enjoying chocolate ice cream cones. "It's my favorite part of the day."

"Really?" asked David. "I didn't know that."

"See, it helps me ease some of the tension I have at school," said Courtney. "You know, helps me unwind. Makes me feel really better."

"Oh, I get the picture," said David.

"I'm glad you do," said Courtney.

Suddenly the white BMW sped into the dairy bar, and the six girls got out of the car.

"Hey, look, girls," said Carla. "David and Courtney are moonlighting."

"Why don't you all just leave David alone?" suggested Courtney, in a state of anger.

"David's our shining star," said Jennifer. "He keeps all of us smiling."

"You all really think so," said Courtney.

"Yes, we think so," said Latish. "We wouldn't be here if he didn't."

"That's only because you all pick on him almost always," said Courtney.

"We don't pick on him," said Carla. "We like him."

"Hey, let's get us some ice cream," said Brittany.

"That's a great idea," said Leandra.

The six problem girls then ordered ice cream, while David and Courtney carried on with their ice cream treat.

"I can't believe they lied on me like that," said David.

"It'll be okay, David," said Courtney.

"Not if they keep lying on me," said David.

"Trust me, David," said Courtney, "everything will be okay."

Later that afternoon, at Keisha's house, Keisha was doing her homework when her mother walked in. She wanted to talk to Keisha about the homecoming ceremonies.

"Hey Keisha?" asked her mother, "we need to talk."

"About what?" asked Keisha.

"Is it true that you're running for prom queen?" asked her mother.

"How did you find that out?" asked Keisha.

"David's younger sister told me," said her mother.

"Well, I was going to surprise you with that," said Keisha.

"If you do decide to run for prom queen," said her mother, "you're going to be a very special one."

"That's right," said Keisha. "And besides, mostly everyone at Canaby High School, especially the entire student body, is happy for me running for prom queen."

"Well, they've got every reason to be," said her mother.

"See, the reason I'm running for prom queen," said Keisha, "is because I'm trying to send a message that a dark childhood and painful emotional scars don't have to destroy your beauty and popularity."

"Well, I'm sure it will all work out," said her mother. "Besides, there are lots of other teenagers with painful childhoods and emotional scars all across the country that have gone on to succeed in life."

"But how many have been chosen as homecoming queen, prom queen, or prom king?" asked Keisha.

"Keisha, I'm not saying that you shouldn't run," said her mother. "If you do decide to run and you get the title, you'll be a very special prom queen."

"Thanks mom," said Keisha. "That's just what I wanted to hear."

"And I'm very proud of you for running for prom queen," said her mother.

"Thanks, mom," said Keisha. "You're the best mother in the world."

Keisha then gave her mother a big hug.

"I hope David's proud of me, too," said Keisha.

"I'm sure he is," said her mother.

Meanwhile, at David's house, his parents were watching television in the living room when David arrived at home.

"Hey, I'm home," said David.

David's mom and dad then found him.

"David, your girlfriend's mom called earlier," said his dad.

"Well, what did she want?" asked David.

"She wanted to talk to you about something," said his dad.

"About what?" asked David.

"She and Keisha say you got upset at school today," said his mother.

"I'd better call Keisha," said David.

David then went into his room, and called Keisha.

"Hello," said Keisha.

"Is Keisha there?" asked David.

"Speaking," said Keisha.

"Keisha, I'm returning a call that was placed here this afternoon," said David.

"Well, I called you earlier," said Keisha, "because I'm thinking about the two of us going out to look at the stars in the sky tonight."

"Do you mean, like, a stargazing trip?" asked David.

"That's right," said Keisha. "How does that sound?"

"That sounds great," said David.

"Okay," said Keisha. "I'll pick you up at nine o' clock."

"Okay," said David. "Bye, Keisha."

"Bye, David," said Keisha.

David then hung up the phone, and saw Robbie standing in his doorway.

"Is there something you want, Robbie?" asked David.

"How did it go?" asked Robbie.

"How did what go?" asked David.

"The phone call to Keisha," said Robbie.

"It went okay," said David.

"So, did you have an emotional breakdown at school today?" asked Robbie.

"Yes, I did," said David. "Why?"

"Because I'm very happy for you for trying out for prom queen," said Robbie.

"Thank you, Robbie," said David.

Just then Robbie walked into David's room.

"So, I heard she's trying out to be the prom queen," said Robbie.

"How did you find that out?" asked David.

"A classmate of mine told me," said Robbie.

"Well, you're right," said David. "She is trying out for prom queen."

"Well, I wish her good luck," said Robbie.

"I'll tell her that," said David.

"Thank you, David," said Robbie.

Keisha may be able to send a message that painful emotional scars and a dark childhood don't have to destroy a child's beauty or popularity by trying out to be the prom queen of her senior class, but she and David happen to be two very special students at Canaby High School.

SIX

That night, Keisha and David went to a quiet park in Rankin County, to look at the stars in the sky. While they were stargazing, Keisha started her quest to be the prom queen of her Senior class.

"I'm really sorry I upset you at school today," said Keisha.

"It's okay," said David, "but I was the one who created a scene in the cafeteria."

"No, David," said Keisha. "It was all my fault."

"How was it your fault when I ran out of the cafeteria?" asked David.

"I was the one who started it," said Keisha. "See, I discussed my dark, miserable childhood, which I normally don't do, and it got you frustrated."

"That's right, Keisha," said David. "But it happened to me, too, and my experience was a lot worse."

"I know it was," said Keisha, "but it will be okay. I promise you it will. Okay?"

"Well, okay," said David.

"Let's talk about something else," said Keisha, "like my effort to be the prom queen."

"Well, we talked about it in the cafeteria," said David.

"I know that," said Keisha, "but this is a chance for you and me to talk about it together."

"Well, okay," said David. "But like I said, just try to follow your heart."

"It's going to mean a lot to me," said Keisha.

"And it'll mean something to me, too," said David.

"I mean, I'm going to be this beautiful girl with emotional scars," said Keisha, "that was physically and sexually abused as a child, just like you were."

"That's right, Keisha," said David.

"I'll have the queen's crown on, and you'll be by my side the whole night," said Keisha. "Won't it be wonderful?" she then asked him.

"Yes, it would," said David. "But it's going to be really, really embarrassing if people were to talk about us during the prom."

"I don't think anyone will talk about us," said Keisha.

"But what if it happens?" asked David.

"I don't think it'll happen," said Keisha. "Besides, mostly all the students will be happy for me trying out for prom queen."

"Well, I hope they are," said David. "At least I am."

"See, I'm trying to send a message with my effort to be the prom queen," said Keisha.

"What kind of message are you trying to send?" asked David.

"That a dark childhood past and emotional scars don't have to destroy your beauty or popularity," said Keisha.

"I don't think your beauty or popularity is destroyed at all," said David. "I mean, you're still beautiful to me, whether you run for prom queen or not."

"Thank you, David," said Keisha.

"And you're really popular at Canaby High School," said David. "I told you that before."

"Thank you, David," said Keisha. "That really helps my feelings a lot."

A while later, the stars in the sky were shining brightly, as Keisha and David were sitting on top of the car, stargazing and sharing a conversation at the same time.

"The stars look beautiful tonight," said Keisha.

"Yeah, Keisha," said David. "They do."

"I wish they could look like this every night," said Keisha.

"Yeah, me too," said David.

"There's even a full moon out tonight," said Keisha.

"I didn't know that," said David. "I guess I came out on a really good night."

"Me too," said Keisha.

The full moon was shining brightly as Keisha and David were holding hands while stargazing.

"David, aren't you happy that we're together tonight?" asked Keisha.

"Yes," said David. "I couldn't be any happier."

"I'm so glad," said Keisha, "because there's this nice slow song that I have in my CD collection that I would like for you and me to slow-dance to."

"Really?" asked David.

"Yes," said Keisha. "Besides, this will help us practice for the big prom night, in case I do get elected."

"That'll be great," said David.

Keisha then went to her car, and put the slow song on. Then she and David started slow-dancing to the song.

"I wish tonight were prom night," said Keisha.

"It'll be here soon," said David. "After all, Spring has barely started."

"I know it's the start of March," said Keisha, "but I'm just nervous about being the prom queen."

"There's no need to be nervous about it," said David. "Besides, we're practicing right now."

Just then Rosalynn stopped by the park. She then got out of her car, and started watching Keisha and David slow-dancing.

"Isn't that so sweet?" asked Rosalynn. "Keisha and David showing their love for each other."

Keisha and David then noticed Rosalynn at the park, and stopped dancing. The song was almost over.

"Rosalynn, what are you doing down here?" asked Keisha.

"I heard you and David were down here," said Rosalynn.

"We were looking at the stars," said Keisha.

"I saw you two doing more than looking at the stars," said Rosalynn.

"We were also practicing for prom night," said David.

"Oh, I see," said Rosalynn. "Well, I heard what happened at school today."

"We've got it taken care of now," said David.

"That's good to hear," said Rosalynn. "I'll just leave now. Good night."

"Good night, Rosalynn," said Keisha.

Rosalynn then got into her car, and left the park as Keisha and David looked on while holding hands.

The next morning at school, the entire campus was packed with students that were waiting for school to begin. David was near the gym when Keisha showed up.

"Hello, David," said Keisha.

"Keisha, I really enjoyed spending time with you last night," said David.

"I'm glad you did," said Keisha. "After a really hectic day yesterday, I felt that we needed to spend some time together."

Keisha and David then walked into the school building. The halls were noisy and crowded.

"David, can I ask you something?" asked Keisha.

"Yes, you can, Keisha," said David.

"After what happened between us last night," said Keisha, "can you look me in the eyes and say that we really and truly deserve each other?"

"Yes, I can," said David.

"That's just what I wanted to hear," said Keisha.

Keisha and David then kissed each other.

"I'll see you later, David," said Keisha.

"Bye, Keisha," said David.

Keisha and David headed to class. Unfortunately, one of the six problem girls was eavesdropping against Keisha and David by hiding behind one of the lockers in the hallway.

"Keisha and David are not going anywhere," said Leandra. "I'm going to see to that."

Leandra ran off to find her friends. The conversation between Keisha and David was now at risk of becoming the talk of the school. But Keisha and David knew that it would all be okay.

SEVEN

Later that morning, in the principal's office, the principal, assistant principal, and secretary were all discussing plans for the senior prom at Canaby High School, which were to begin with the prom queen elections.

"I think it's time to find our prom queen for this year," said the principal.

"Well, the elections aren't until Monday night," said the secretary.

"I know that," said the principal, "but the runners have to fill out a form. And I'm taking care of that today."

"When are the forms due?" asked the assistant principal.

"At the end of the school day tomorrow," said the principal.

At that moment the principal turned on the intercom and made the announcement.

"Okay, may I have your attention, please?" asked the principal, speaking through the intercom. "Those of you twelfth-grade girls that are planning on trying out for prom queen need to come by the office either today or tomorrow and fill out a form. The qualifications for prom queen are: you must have grades of seventy or better in all of your classes, and your citizenship must be no lower than a 'C.' The deadline is the end of the school day tomorrow. Remember, you must be a twelfth-grade girl in order to fill out a prom queen form."

When morning break came, Keisha was headed to the office to fill out a form for prom queen when Michael found her. The halls were noisy and crowded.

"Hey Keisha?" he asked.

"What is it, Michael?" asked Keisha.

"Congratulations on running for prom queen," said Michael.

"Thank you, Michael," said Keisha.

"Anyway, there's a rumor going around the school about you and David," said Michael.

"What kind of rumor?" asked Keisha.

Meanwhile, Jenny and Kerry were in the hallway talking about the rumor going around about Keisha and David.

"I don't believe this," said Kerry. "First, those girls pick on David continuosly, and now they choose to talk about him behind his back."

"I sure hope Courtney's aware of it," said Jenny.

"But we're his best friends," said Kerry. "We should be looking out for him, not putting him down."

"David is going to be frustrated when he becomes aware of this," said Jenny.

"But what if he's already aware of it?" asked Kerry.

"What if he loses his cool?" asked Jenny.

"What if he gets into a fight?" asked Kerry.

At that moment Jenny and Kerry started to fear for David.

"We gotta find David!" shrieked both Jenny and Kerry.

Jenny and Kerry then ran to try to find David. Meanwhile, Keisha became frustrated when she found out about the rumor.

"I can't believe this," said Keisha. "Those six girls have gone too far by spreading rumors about me and David."

"I'm telling you," said Michael, "you ought to go to the principal about this."

"Okay, if you think it will work for me," said Keisha, "I'll give it a try."

Meanwhile, David was at the snack bar, enjoying a jelly doughnut and soda when he noticed a huge group of girls talking about him and Keisha. He hurried out of the snack bar, and into the hallway to snap at them. Fortunately, Latasha stopped him.

"Hey David?" asked Latasha.

"What is it, Latasha?" asked David.

"I wouldn't fight them if I were you," said Latasha.

"Thanks for telling me that," said David, "but I'm not going to let them damage my reputation like this."

"Well, well, well," said a girl in the group. "It looks like Mr. Screwup is finally talking."

"You'd better watch who you call Mr. Screwup," said David.

"David, please don't create a scene," said Latasha.

"I'm trying not to," said David.

"Well, it looks like you will," said another girl in the group.

"Why don't you all leave him alone?" suggested Latasha.

"We're his worst nightmare," said the second girl.

"David, please don't let them get to you," said Latasha.

Just then Jenny and Kerry found David.

"David, please don't lose your cool," said Jenny. "Okay?"

"Please don't create a scene, David," said Kerry.

"I'm trying not to," said David.

"I think he'll be okay," said Latasha.

Just then Keisha found David, and ran up to him.

"David, are you okay?" asked Keisha.

"I'm fine, Keisha," said David.

While chaos was going on between Keisha and David—and lots of other students were wondering what was going on, David wasn't paying attention to his snacks. Carla was eating his jelly doughnut and drinking his soda while smiling at the situation David was in.

"I wish you all would just let David be," said Keisha.

"David, are you sure you're going to be okay?" asked Jenny.

"I think I can make it," said David.

"David, why don't you just go on to class?" suggested Latasha. "Okay?"

"Yeah, David," said Kerry. "Just go on to class."

"Well, okay," said David.

David then went into the snack bar for his snacks, only to find that Carla ate them. She laughed at him, and he got really angry and tempered.

"You ate my snacks!" yelled David.

Carla kept laughing at David, and Keisha, Jenny, Kerry, Latasha, and several other concerned students became worried about David.

"David," said Kerry.

"This girl ate my snacks!" yelled David.

"That's what you get for trying to fight us," said the first girl.

Lots of girls outside the snack bar started laughing, as students inside the snack bar, including Latasha's friends, were shocked. Keisha then went into the snack bar.

"David, don't let them get to you," said Keisha.

"Like I said, I'm trying not to," said David.

"Why don't you let me walk you to class?" suggested Keisha, "okay, David?"

"Well, okay," said David.

Keisha then walked David to class, in front of everyone.

"I knew it," said Jenny. "I knew someone was out to trouble David."

Just then the principal, in a state of anger, rushed out into the hallway.

"What is going on out here?" he asked.

"Someone tried to trouble David," said Kerry.

Meanwhile, Keisha was comforting David outside his class.

"David, I'm very happy that you handled your frustrations out there," said Keisha.

"But that doesn't make me feel better," said David.

"David, I know you're frustrated about being picked on like that," said Keisha, "but I promise you that one day, you're the one that's going to get the last laugh."

"Thank you, Keisha," said David.

"I'll save a seat for you in the cafeteria," said Keisha.

"Thank you, Keisha," said David. "I'll see you at lunchtime."

"Bye, David," said Keisha.

David then took his seat in the U.S. History class when Courtney greeted him.

"Hi, David," she said.

"Hello, Courtney," said David.

"Are you feeling better?" asked Courtney.

"Not really," said David.

"Why?" asked Courtney.

"Because I almost got into a fight," said David.

"It'll be okay," said Courtney. "I promise."

Meanwhile, in the office, the assistant principal and secretary were going over prom queen forms that had already been filled out. Keisha had already filled hers out, too.

"Okay, we've got eleven girls running for prom queen so far," said the assistant principal.

"And I see Keisha is one of them," said the assistant principal.

"That's right," said the assistant principal. "Her form is right here."

The assistant principal then showed the secretary Keisha's form for prom queen.

"Oh, I see," said the secretary. "Well, I wish her good luck."

"I wish her good luck, too," said the assistant principal.

Just then the principal, in a state of anger, walked in.

"I feel sorry for all of those girls that have teased, picked on, provoked, harassed, and made fun of David Malone all this time," said David.

"What are you talking about?" asked the assistant principal.

"A huge number of girls went teasing and making fun of David in the hallway," said the principal. "And Carla Simpson even ate his morning break snacks in the snack bar. All because his girlfriend is running for prom queen."

"Well, Keisha's form is right here," said the secretary.

The secretary then showed the principal Keisha's form.

"I believe most of the school is supporting Keisha in her prom queen campaign," said the assistant principal.

"You know, Keisha will make a very special prom queen," said the principal, "because, as children, she and David Malone were abused, raped, and beaten, both physically and sexually. And they both ended up in foster homes in several states. Back then, their chances of succeeding in life, as well as graduating from high school, were very, very slim."

"Well, they've turned all that around," said the assistant principal, "because they're both straight-A students, in several school clubs, and Senior Class Favorites for this year."

"You know, I think that Keisha should be elected prom queen," said the secretary, "and that you should choose David as the prom king."

"Well, maybe it will happen," said the principal.

Later that afternoon, in the school library, Keisha was working on her prom queen campaign fliers when Latasha walked into the library.

"Hey Keisha?" asked Latasha.

"What is it Latasha?" asked Keisha.

"Good luck on your campaign," said Latasha.

"Thank you, Latasha," said Keisha.

"Even my friends are happy for you," said Latasha.

Just then several of Latasha's friends walked into the library.

"Hey, Keisha," said Cheryl.

"Hey, Cheryl," said Keisha.

"We're really happy for you for trying out for prom queen," said Cheryl.

"I think you make an excellent prom queen," said Ronnie.

"Thank you, Ronnie," said Keisha. "I really need that."

"Well, you have my vote for prom queen, too," said Cheryl.

"The elections are Monday night," said Latasha.

Just then a student named Laura walked into the library.

"Hey Latasha?" she asked, "we need to talk."

"About what?" asked Latasha.

"About Keisha running for prom queen," said Laura. "Do you know that other students are making fun of her and David because of this prom queen thing?" she then asked.

"Yes," said Ronnie. "Everyone's aware of it."

"I mean, I'm happy for Keisha, too," said Laura, "but I just don't think it's fair for Keisha and David to be known laughingstocks because of all this."

"Thank you, Laura," said Keisha.

"Keisha's got my vote, too," said Laura.

"I'll tell everyone to vote for Keisha for prom queen," said Latasha.

"That's very sweet of you," said Keisha.

"Bye, Keisha," said Latasha. "And good luck."

At that moment Latasha and her friends left the library, and Keisha continued to work on her fliers. Her chances of getting the prom queen title remained good at that very moment.

EIGHT

When it came time for spring break, Keisha and her mother were packing their suitcases. They were planning to take a vacation to the Mississippi Gulf Coast for a week on the beach. While Keisha was packing her bags, her mother walked into her room.

"Hey Keisha?" asked her mother.

"What is it, mom?" asked Keisha.

"Would you like to bring David along?" asked her mother.

"I'd love to," said Keisha.

"Well, go call him and ask him," said her mother.

Keisha then went to the phone and called David. However, his mother answered the phone. David and his sister Robbie were watching a movie on television.

"Hello," said his mother.

"Can I speak to David?" asked Keisha.

"Just a minute," said his mother. "Hey David, telephone."

Just then David went to the phone.

"Hello," said David.

"Hey, David," said Keisha. "My mom and I are taking a spring break vacation to the Mississippi Gulf Coast, and we were wondering if you wanted to come along."

And sure enough, David agreed. Later that day, Keisha, her mother, and David were all headed to Biloxi for a week on the coastal waters. They took U.S. Highway 49 South from the Jackson area, all the way to the Mississippi Gulf Coast, passing through towns such as Mendenhall, Magee, Mt. Olive, and Collins. They also passed through the city of Hattiesburg.

When they got to the town of Wiggins, Keisha's mom, who was driving the car, pulled off of the highway, and got out of the car.

Keisha, who was looking at a magazine, was sitting in the back seat next to David, who was sleep.

"Are you okay, David?" asked Keisha.

"I'm fine," whispered David. "I'm just sleepy."

Meanwhile, Keisha's mom was standing, leaning on the back of the car when Keisha got out of the car. Lots of cars and trucks were traveling on U.S. 49 South near the Highway 26 exit, where they were parked.

"Is everything okay, mom?" asked Keisha.

"Yes, Keisha," said her mother. "I'm just taking a little break from driving."

"Well, okay," said Keisha.

Keisha and her mother then got back into the car, and it got back on the highway. Soon, Keisha, her mother, and David were in Gulfport. When they got to Biloxi, they checked into the Broadwater Beach Resort and Marina. When they got to their room at the hotel, they were very, very happy.

"Isn't this nice, Keisha?" asked her mother.

"Yes, mom," said Keisha. "It is nice. It feels really, really good in here because of the air conditioning."

"Do you think David will enjoy this vacation?" asked her mother.

"I'm sure he will," said Keisha. "I know why they call it spring break."

"Why?" asked her mother.

"So you can have fun on the coastal waters," said Keisha.

Just then David, carrying his suitcase, walked into the room. He was very worn out from the long ride.

"Are you okay, David?" asked Keisha.

"Yes, Keisha," said David. "I'm just tired."

"Well, I'm sure you'll feel better soon," said Keisha's mother.

"Yeah, maybe so," said David.

Just then David got on the bed, and began lying down.

"David, I'm sure you're going to have fun here on the coast," said Keisha's mother.

"I hope so," said David, "because I wasn't planning on taking a spring break vacation."

"Well, consider it a surprise, David," said Keisha.

Later that afternoon, on the beach, there was a huge beach party taking place. There were lots of teenagers and young adults at the party having fun. Music was playing, refreshments were being served, and the mid-afternoon flow of traffic on U.S. Highway 90 was very heavy. Lots of pedestrians coming from the Broadwater Beach Resort and Marina to go to the beach were waiting to cross the street. Meanwhile, Keisha and David, who had their beach accessories with them, were headed to the beach.

"Keisha, I really wanna thank you and your mom for bringing me along on this trip," said David.

"It's no problem," said Keisha. "Besides, I'm really glad that you're here on this trip."

"Yeah, Keisha," said David. "So am I."

"David, I'll bet that when school resumes Monday," said Keisha, "we'll be able to say that we had the most wonderful spring break."

"Yeah, Keiaha," said David. "Maybe so."

When Keisha and David got to the U.S. 90 crosswalk, traffic was stopped, as their light was on red, and Keisha and David crossed the street with no problem. When they got to the beach, they saw part of the huge beach party that was taking place.

"What's going on over there?" asked David.

"They're probably having a beach party," said Keisha. "But let's not interfere with them. Okay?"

"Well, okay," said David.

The fact that there was, indeed, a beach party taking place didn't stop Keisha and David. They went to a more quieter place on the beach. Throughout the afternoon, they did a number of wonderful things together on the beach, such as swimming in the beach water, playing in the sand, participating in a volleyball game, building sand castles, and playing frisbee.

Around seven o' clock, as the sun was going down, traffic on U.S. 90 had slowed down, and Keisha and David were heading back to the hotel after a fun afternoon on the beach.

"Did you have fun today?" asked Keisha.

"Yes, Keisha," said David. "I had a lot of fun."

"I'll bet that we've already got something to remember spring break by," said Keisha.

"Yeah, me, too," said Keisha.

A few days later, at a steak house in Rankin County, the six problem girls were meeting in the banquet room, discussing a plan to stop Keisha from running for prom queen. The steak house was crowded.

"Keisha and David both have criminal records," said Carla, "and they're still being hailed as likely to succeed."

"Well, maybe they're so popular at Canaby High School," said Latish.

"But still, their criminal records are going to haunt them for the rest of their lives," said Jennifer.

"Keisha may be popular at Canaby High School," said Carla, "but after next week, she can forget about being the prom queen. All thanks to us."

"So, how do we bring her prom queen run to an end?" asked Leandra.

"Like this," said Carla.

Carla then showed her friends a dangerous and slanderous plan to stop Keisha's prom queen run. Carla explained the plan clearly, as Jennifer, Latish, Leandra, Brittany, and Melanie listened carefully. Lots of other patrons were overseeing what was going on.

"If we follow this simple plan and it works," said Carla, "then we will have robbed Keisha of her run for prom queen."

"We're all in," said Brittany.

Just then a patron approached Carla, and Carla turned around.

"Shouldn't you be happy for Keisha like everyone else?" asked the patron. She then jabbed Carla in the face, and everyone in the restaurant, including the other five problem girls, were stunned.

"You're going to be sorry you hit her!" yelled Brittany.

The other four problem girls became belligerent, and quickly reacted. Brittany pointed a .22 Revolver at several patrons, while Jennifer pointed a .357 Magnum at some child and teenage patrons."

"Put your hands up, everyone!" shouted Jennifer.

"Why should we?" asked a teenage boy.

"You all better do what she says," said Brittany.

"Please don't hurt us!" cried a child at the restaurant.

"Shut up!" shouted Carla.

"Put your hands up," said Jennifer.

The restaurant patrons helplessly obeyed the girls, and then Carla grabbed her handgun.

"They're going to kill someone!" shrieked a teenage girl.

"Shut up!" yelled Brittany.

"Please don't hurt us!" cried another child.

"Don't you all know what shut up means?" yelled Jennifer.

Just then the restaurant manager saw what was happening.

"Oh, my god," she said. "My banquet room's been robbed. Those kids have weapons."

"Who are you all calling kids?" asked Melanie.

"You all ought to be ashamed of yourselves," said the restaurant manager.

"Well, we're not," said Carla, "and there's no one to stop us."

"Oh, yes, there is," said Rosalynn.

Rosalynn then came into the banquet room, and began wrestling the gun out of Carla's hand. As lots of patrons began hurrying out of the banquet room, Brittany fired a shot into the air, causing everyone inside the restaurant to start screaming. Soon after, Brittany started shooting whichever way she could. As a direct result, several people were injured, and most of the restaurant property was damaged.

A while later, several police officers were traveling down Interstate 20 East, between the Terry Road and Interstate 55 exits. They were responding to the criminal complaint that the restaurant manager had filed. When they got to the restaurant, which was located on U.S. Highway 80 at the end of U.S. Highway 49 just after Interstate 20 in Pearl, they saw lots of restaurant patrons standing outside the building in a state of fear. The police officers got everyone under control.

"Hey, let's settle down here," said one of the police officers.

"The six girls that shot at us are in there," said a restaurant patron.

"Well, they are going to be out of your way shortly," said another police officer.

Just then an ambulance arrived at the restaurant, and several ambulance workers began carrying a stretcher into the restaurant.

"Okay, where's the injured person?" asked an ambulance worker.

"There are several injured people here," said a third police officer. He then radioed for more ambulances.

"We need a couple more ambulances," the police officer said through his walkie-talkie.

Just then the manager showed up outside the restaurant.

"Thank god you all are here," said the manager. "Here's what happened. A group of six girls threatened my patrons with guns."

"Wait a second," said a fourth police officer, "did you just mention guns?"

"Yes, I did," said the manager.

"That's a deadly weapon," said the same police officer.

Meanwhile, inside the restaurant, a twelve-year-old girl was comforting an eleven-year-old boy who was so traumatized that he was crying.

"It's okay," said the girl. "It wasn't your fault. You didn't do anything wrong."

"I might have nightmares from this," said the boy.

"You probably won't have nightmares," said the girl. "Those girls that opened fire are the ones responsible for all this."

Just then the girl and boy both heard a detective reading the six problem girls their Miranda rights.

"You six young ladies have got the right to remain silent," said the detective. "Anything you all say can and will be used against you in a court of law."

Just then the girl and boy saw several police officers and the detective leading the six problem girls, all in handcuffs, out of the building.

"You all have the right to attorneys," said the detective. "For those of you who cannot afford one, one will be appointed for you. Do you all understand these rights?"

A few minutes later, the manager, who was still outside the building, was notified of the criminal charges brought against the six girls.

"Okay, here are the charges," said the detective. "Aggravated assault and battery, carrying deadly weapons on public property, and disturbing the peace."

"Thank you," said the manager. "Thank you very much."

Later that night, Keisha and David were watching a movie on television while lying on the first bed.

"Are you okay, David?" asked Keisha.

"Kind of," said David. "But I'm kind of sleepy."

"I tell you what," said Keisha. "Why don't you go outside and buy a soda?" she then suggested. "Okay?"

"Well, okay," said David.

David then went outside to the vending machines to enjoy his soda. While he was enjoying his soda, Keisha called him, having found out about the Rankin County steak house incident.

"Hey David?" asked Keisha.

"Yes, what is it, Keisha?" asked David.

"Those six girls that keep harassing us are in jail in Jackson for carrying concealed weapons on public property, disturbing the peace, and aggravated assault and battery," said Keisha.

When Keisha and David got back to the hotel room, they saw the incident on the news.

"According to Jackson Police," said the news anchor, on television, "six teenage girls from Canaby walked into the Western Sizzlin on U.S. Highway 80 in Pearl and threatened several restaurant patrons."

Video from the incident then came on the screen.

"Three patrons were shot by the girls while trying to foil a would-be plot to damage the prom queen campaign of Canaby High School senior Keisha Blackledge."

"I knew it," said Keisha. "I knew they were trying to get back at me."

"Keisha, it's not your fault," said David.

"I know," said Keisha, "but they have gone too far by wrecking my prom queen campaign."

"Well, they are only hurting themselves by messing up your prom queen campaign," said David.

"I can't keep letting them do this to me," said Keisha. "If I don't get

the prom queen title, it's gonna mess my whole year up."

"Keisha, just report it to the principal Monday," said David.

"Okay, I'll do just that," said Keisha.

Throughout the rest of the spring break, Keisha and David went to the beach more often, and they went to several spots on the coast, such as Beauvoir, the last home of Jefferson Davis, Marine Life, where they saw a dolphin show, went shopping and hung out at the Edgewater Mall on one occasion. One night, they drove down U.S. 90, passing by several restaurants, hotels, and shopping centers. The night lights all over Biloxi and Gulfport, especially along U.S. 90, looked very bright and beautiful, and the moon was shining brightly.

On another occasion, Keisha and David went to a cinema on the coast to see a movie. They saw a romantic comedy, and shared a kiss while enjoying popcorn and sodas. They went out to eat at the Blow-Fry Inn restaurant that evening, and enjoyed a wonderful seafood dinner. Later that night, they went to Fun Time USA, where they played goofy golf, rode in the water bumper cars, and played video games in the arcade. They even enjoyed refreshments while at the amusement park. Sure enough, Keisha and David had a spring break that they would never forget.

NINE

The week after spring break, on the school campus, the outside of the school was filled with students, most of whom were experiencing "Prom Fever," as the big night was drawing near. The main hallway of the school, which was also noisy and packed, was surrounded with posters, fliers, and banners by prom queen candidates. When David arrived at school that Monday morning, he saw Keisha's huge flier.

"I'll be glad when Keisha wins this thing," he said.

Just then Jenny and Kerry found David.

"David, are you okay?" asked Jenny.

"No, I am not," said David. "Not at all."

"David, we heard about what happened over spring break," said Kerry.

"I know," said David. "I cannot keep letting those girls hurt Keisha's prom queen chances."

"We'll notify the principal about all this, okay?" asked Jenny.

"Well, okay," said David.

"I tell you what, David," said Kerry, "sit with us at lunch today, and we'll talk about it."

Later that morning, in the choir room, the school choir was practicing on a song that they would be performing for an upcoming concert. While most of the 150 choir members were girls, Keisha, David, Jenny, and Kerry were all choir members. When the choir conductor heard a mistake in the song, he stopped everyone from singing.

"Stop the song, everybody," he said.

The entire choir room was then quiet.

"We have got to get this song right," said the conductor. "This is one of the songs that we will perform at the Mississippi Coliseum on May 19. So we need to practice on this piece really well."

"How many songs are we gonna sing?" asked a choir member.

"Probably about four or five," said the choir member.

At that moment the cell phone of a choir member rang, and she answered it.

"Hello," she said.

The rest of the choir was wondering what was going on.

"Just a minute," she said. "David, it's for you."

She then handed the cell phone to David.

"Hello," he said.

"Hello, David," said the voice on the other end of the phone. "I just called to inform you that you won't be sitting with Jenny and Kerry in the cafeteria today."

"Excuse me," said David.

"I mean, you'll be dead by lunch time," said the phone party. "I'm going to see to that."

David then hung up the phone, and started panicking.

"Are you okay, David?" asked Keisha.

"David, what's the matter?" asked the choir conductor.

The rest of the choir was wondering what was going on.

"Keisha, someone's trying to hire a hit man to kill me," said David.

"What?" cried Keisha. "Are you sure?"

The rest of the choir members started panicking.

"That's what the person on the phone said," said David.

"Then it could be those six girls that keep harassing you," said Keisha.

"Wait a minute," said the choir member with the cell phone. "Who keeps harassing David?"

"There's a clique of six girls that give David nothing but trouble," said Keisha.

"I've heard of those girls," said the choir member with the cell phone, whose name was Shanna. "All they do is cause trouble. All they do is try to wreck other students' chances of gaining popularity."

"That's right," said another choir member. "A number of girls that have run for prom queen in the past have lost their campaigns at the expense of those girls."

"Excuse me, everybody," said David.

David then walked out of the choir room.

"All of you are right," said the choir conductor. "David doesn't deserve to be treated like this."

Meanwhile, David was leaning on a soda machine in the hallway when Shanna spotted him.

"Hey David?" she asked.

"Yeah, what do you want?" asked David.

"Don't blame yourself for all this," said Shanna. "It's not your fault."

"I'm not blaming myself for anything," said David.

"David, I'm happy for Keisha for running for prom queen," said Shanna, "and I'm happy for you for supporting her."

"That's sweet of you," said David, "but my life is in danger here."

"David, I'm happy for you," said Shanna.

"I know that," said David, "but now they're trying to have me killed. And I haven't done anything to them at all. None whatsoever."

"I promise you, David," said Shanna, "I'm not going to let them hurt you or Keisha."

"Thanks," said David. "That's very sweet of you."

David then gave Shanna a big hug.

"Anytime you need to talk to someone," said Shanna, "you can talk to me."

"Okay," said David. "I'll keep that in mind."

Just then Keisha showed up in the hallway.

"Is everything okay?" she asked.

"Yes, Keisha," said Shanna. "I comforted him, and made him feel better."

"That's sweet of you, Shanna," said David.

"I'm hoping that you win the prom queen title," said Shanna, "and that the principal chooses David as the prom king. I'm even going to help you win the title at the elections tonight."

"Really?" asked David.

"Yes," said Shanna. "In fact, I truly think that the two of you make an excellent couple."

"That's very sweet of you," said Keisha. "Are you okay, David."

"Yes," said David. "I'm okay."

"That's good to hear," said Keisha.

Around the lunch hour, the halls were crowded as lots of students were looking forward to the elections for prom queen to be held that night. Posters, fliers, and banners of prom queen candidates were decorated all over the hallways.

While Latasha and some of her friends were talking about the big night, a number of other students that were part of another student's prom queen campaign started boasting about Keisha's campaign.

"Well, well, well," said a student named Terry. "It looks like Melinda's got some competition tonight at the elections."

"Yes, it sure does," said Latasha. "If Miss Melinda wants to be the prom queen, she'll have to get past Keisha Blackledge."

"And that won't be hard for her at all," said a student named Steve.

"I think it will be," said Latasha.

"Yeah," said a student named Gregory, "that's what you think. But believe me, Melinda's gonna walk away with it all."

Just then Melinda showed up in the hallway.

"Well, how are those pamphlets coming along?" she asked.

"I hope you know that Keisha has a better chance than you," said Ronnie.

"Oh, Keisha's not going to win this thing," said Melinda. "I'm going to win it all."

"What if we told you that you don't stand a chance?" asked Latasha.

"Yeah," said Cheryl. "What if we told you that you just don't have what it takes?"

"She's got every chance in the world," said Paulette.

She then handed out the phony pamphlets to Latasha and her friends.

"That details it all," said Jodi. "Have a nice day, and remember to vote for Melinda tonight."

Latasha and her friends read the phony card, and immediately took action.

"No!" cried Latasha. "They can't do this to her."

"Latasha, it's okay," said Cheryl.

"This is not okay," said Latasha. "When Keisha sees this, she's going to freak out."

"Latasha, everything's going to be all right," said Ronnie.

"Yeah, Ronnie," said Brianna. "As long as you vote for Melinda."

"If Keisha doesn't get to be prom queen," said Cheryl, "I'm going to hold all of you responsible."

"And wouldn't that be great?" asked Jodi. "For me and David to start dating."

"Jodi, you and David are not going to be girlfriend and boy-friend,"

said Ronnie. "Do you get the picture?"

"Well you must be living in a fantasy world," said Jodi.

"No, Jodi," said Ronnie. "You're the one that's probably living in a fantasy world."

"No, you're the one that's living in a fantasy world," said Jodi.

"How dare you, Jodi," said Ronnie.

"Ronnie, please don't let her get to you," said Cheryl. "Okay?"

Meanwhile, in the cafeteria, Keisha, David, Jenny, Kerry, and Shanna were talking about the prom queen elections while enjoying the

lunch hour. The cafeteria, which was crowded, was having hot, juicy T-bone steak, texas toast, and baked potatoes for lunch.

"Will there ever come a time during this prom queen campaign where me and Keisha can feel good about thinking of prom night without being embarrassed?" asked David.

"David, we know you're frustrated because Carla Simpson and her friends tried to harm Keisha's campaign," said Kerry, "but just try not to make such a big deal out of it."

"David, let me share a secret with you," said Shanna. "Okay?"

"What secret?" asked David, in a state of anger.

"Every other girl has fallen victim to Carla and her friends in the

past when they were running for spots on school organizations,"
said Shanna.

"Well, Keisha is not every other girl," said David. "Every other
girl wasn't abused, beaten, and raped as a child, and every other girl
doesn't have a dark and lonely childhood and painful emotional scars."

"Shanna, those girls like to wreck other students' chances of
gaining popularity," said Jenny.

"Can I say something?" asked Keisha.

"You sure can," said Kerry.

"If I don't get chosen as the prom queen," said Keisha, "it's going
to mess up my whole year."

Suddenly Shanna, Jenny, Kerry, David, and Keisha, as well as
lots of other students in the cafeteria, heard bickering and yelling out
in the hallway.

"I wonder what's going on out there," said Shanna. At that moment lots of students went to the door of the cafeteria, where they
then saw Latasha and another student that was helping Melinda with
her campaign arguing over who would make the best prom queen.
The hallway was very crowded.

"Keisha's got a criminal record!" yelled the other student.

"She's gonna be the prom queen!" yelled Latasha.

"How could she when she's been to jail before?" asked the
other student, in a state of anger.

"She's got the whole school supporting her!" yelled Latasha, "and
I'm not about to let anyone ruin it for her."

"Keisha don't got no support!" yelled the other student.

"She's got more support than most of you all believing those fliers
think!" yelled Latasha.

"Screw those fliers!" yelled the other student. "Keisha ain't gonna
get it."

Suddenly Latasha shoved the other student as hard as she could,
and he then shoved her back. Soon, the two were throwing punches
like crazy, right in front of everyone in the hallway. When Jenny and
Kerry saw the fight, they rushed out into the crowded hallway to
break up the fight. Ronnie and Cheryl, who were worried all along,

helped break the fight up by grabbing Latasha's arms. Jenny and a few other students in the hallway that were Latasha's friends, restained the other student as Kerry stepped between Latasha and the other student. Keisha, David, and Shanna were standing out into the hallway in a state of anger.

"You two are only acting like children by fighting like this," said Kerry. "Especially over this prom queen thing."

"He's going around sending phony fliers that could damage Keisha," said Latasha.

"I said Keisha ain't gonna get the title," said the other student.

"Yeah, that's what you think," said Latasha.

"Look, you all don't need to be arguing over who's going to be the prom queen," said Kerry. "That's what the elections are for. When the elections take place tonight, just vote for whoever you want to."

"Why's Keisha running when she's got a criminal record?" asked the other student.

"Because she really deserves to be the queen," said Latasha.

"Latasha, you didn't have to say that," said Keisha.

"Let me give you two a word of advice," said Kerry, "okay?"

"Well, okay," said the other student.

"You two might not vote for the same person for prom queen," said Kerry, "and that's okay. But fighting over it won't make things better. So just don't make such a big deal out of it. Okay?"

"Well, okay," said the other student.

Latasha and the other student shook hands.

"I'm sorry I upset you," said the other student.

"It's okay," said Latasha.

Around eight o' clock that night, on the Canaby High School football field, the elections for prom queen were taking place. The stadium was crowded, as over 2,500 high school, junior college, and college students were cheering with excitement. Sixteen excited prom queen candidates were running. A number of press members from all over Mississippi, including several staff writers from the Jackson Clarion-Ledger newspaper, news crews from three Jackson TV stations, and photographers from all over the state, were covering the huge event. Posters, fliers, and banners filled the stadium. Keisha, Melinda, and the other fourteen candidates were all excited about being the prom queen. But only one could get the crown. Just then the principal quieted the crowd down.

"Okay, may I have your attention, please?" asked the principal. "This year, we have sixteen beautiful young ladies that are running for the title of prom queen. At this time I would like for each candidate to introduce themselves to the large crowd that we have tonight."

Keisha, Melinda, and the other fourteen candidates, all wearing numbers (from 1 to 16) were standing in that order on the stage. The first candidate then picked up a microphone that was laying on a table on the stage, and introduced herself to the crowd.

"Hello, everyone," she said. "I'm prom queen candidate number 1, Bridgette Lowery."

The crowd applauded, and she then gave the microphone to the next candidate, who then introduced herself.

"Hi, everyone," she said. "I'm prom queen candidate number 2, Lacey Williams."

The crowd applauded again, and the microphone was passed down to the next candidate.

"Hello," said the next candidate. "I'm candidate number 3, Tia Jefferies."

The applauding and microphone process continued.

"Hi, everyone," said the next candidate. "I'm prom queen candidate number 4, Lacey Woodham."

The applauding and microphone process continued.

"Hello, I'm candidate number 5, Jennifer Carneal."

The applauding and microphone process continued.

"Hello, everyone, I'm candidate number 6, Tina Rhodes."

The applauding and microphone process continued. But when Melinda, who was candidate number 7, introduced herself to the crowd, Jenny and Kerry were terrified.

"Hello, everyone," said Melinda. "I'm prom queen candidate number 7, Melinda Banta."

"What makes Melinda think she's going to get the prom queen title?" asked Kerry.

"I don't know," said Jenny, "but I'm hoping she doesn't prove us wrong."

Meanwhile, at the prom night elections, Melinda gave the microphone to the next candidate, who then introduced herself.

"Hi, I'm candidate number 8, Laura Hearn."

The applauding and microphone process continued.

"Hi, I'm candidate number 9, Breane Lofton."

The applauding and microphone process continued.

"Hello, I'm prom queen candidate number 10, Stacey Wayne."

Just then Keisha began to get nervous while standing on stage, as lots of students and several of the other prom queen candidates were looking on.

"Hey, what's wrong with her?" asked a candidate.

"I don't know," said another candidate. "She might be depressed."

Meanwhile, David was stunned at what was happening.

"Something's not right," said David.

"It'll be okay, David," said Shanna.

"I've never seen her like that before," said David.

"David, if I were you, I would go up there and try to talk to her," said Rosalynn.

"Rosalynn, he can't do that," said Shanna.

Later at the prom night elections, the fifteenth candidate introduced herself to the crowd.

"Hi, I'm prom queen candidate number 15, Shonda Riley."

The crowd applauded again, and Shonda then gave the microphone to Keisha, who was prom queen candidate number 16. It was her turn to introduce herself.

"You go, Keisha!" yelled David.

Shanna and Rosalynn then complimented him.

"That was amazing," said Shanna.

"How did you learn to do that?" asked Rosalynn.

"I just taught myself," said David. "If you all wanna do it with me, you all can."

"I think we will," said Rosalynn.

David, Shanna, and Rosalynn started cheering Keisha on, followed by Jenny, Kerry, Latasha and her friends, and lots of other classmates. But when mostly the whole crowd was cheering Keisha on, she finally introduced herself.

"Okay, quiet down, everyone," said Keisha. "I'm introducing myself now. I'm candidate number 16, Keisha Blackledge."

Just then the crowd applauded with excitement, and Keisha had a big smile on her face. She was really, really happy.

"Way to go, Keisha," said Keisha.

While most of the crowd was still cheering Keisha on, lots of newspaper photographers were taking pictures, and several news crews were making stories on her success for their late news shows. Keisha, still smiling and holding the microphone, was waving to everyone in the crowd. The excitement of the crowd just might be Keisha's winning ticket to the prom queen title.

TEN

A couple of days later, David and his sister, Robbie, went to the city playground and basketball court in downtown Jackson, just so David could get away from the school atmosphere.

"David, I really feel sorry for those students that are going around teasing and making fun of you and Keisha," said Robbie.

"It is time that someone was really happy for me for a change," said David.

"I've always been happy for you, David," said Robbie.

"I know," said David. "You're my sister, and you care a lot about me."

"That's right," said Robbie. "I'm even hoping that you and Keisha get to be prom queen and prom king."

"I'm really looking forward to prom night," said David.

"That's why I really feel sorry for students that tease and make fun of you," said Robbie.

"I don't think that's your problem, Robbie," said David, "but thanks."

Just then a pickup truck arrived at the park, and nineteen college girls jumped out of the truck, and headed to the basketball court. Ten of the girls played a game of twenty-one, while David, Robbie, and the other nine girls watched. The girls that were playing basketball played very hard. Soon, three more pickup trucks arrived at the park, and when that happened, forty-eight guys and sixty-three girls were at the park. The ten girls on the court stopped their game, and started a new game. In the new game, twenty guys and twenty girls were playing ball on the court, while everyone else, including David and Robbie, was watching. The guys and the girls were playing really hard, and baskets were being shot like crazy. During the game, one of the players threw the ball too high, and it landed where David could catch it. He caught it, and sure enough, shot it. It went through the hoop, and everyone watching the game applauded.

"David, that's was wonderful," said Robbie.

"Thank you, Robbie," said David.

Some of the guys playing ball then complimented him.

"Hey, that was excellent," said one guy.

"Well, thank you," said David.

"David, they're wanting to see you play," said Robbie.

"Yeah, David," said a girl on the court. "We wanna see what you've got."

"All I did was shoot the ball through the hoop," said David.

"David, you ought to play for them," said Robbie.

"Well, okay," said David.

David then went out on the the court, and began playing on the guy's team, while another girl that was at the park went out on the court, and began playing on the girl's team. The game, which was a game of twenty-one, resumed, and Robbie started cheering David on as everyone else continued watching the game.

"Go, David!" yelled Robbie.

Again, the guys and girls played hard, and baskets were being shot like crazy. But while the guys were winning, the girls had no problem whatsoever catching up. When the score became eleven to six in favor of the guys, David got the ball, and tried to throw it to one of his teammates, but most of the girls were all up on him, making him feel uncomfortable. As David, who had both of his hands raised, was still trying to throw the ball, a female spectator snuck onto the court, and tickled his armpits. As David screamed and jumped back, the guys called a time-out. The spectator, who was smiling and giggling, looked at David.

"You're great out there," said the spectator.

"Yeah, I'll bet," said David, "because you really distracted me."

"That's what I love about you," said the spectator. "You're so competitive, so talented, and so ticklish."

"I beg your pardon," said David.

"David, is she bothering you?" asked Robbie.

"It's okay, Robbie," said David.

"He is great on the court," said the spectator.

"You leave my brother alone," said Robbie.

"Robbie, I am okay," said David.

"Are you sure?" asked Robbie.

"I apologize if I offended you," said the spectator.

"I'm okay," said David. "Just don't let it happen again."

"I promise I won't," said the spectator.

Just then the game resumed and the girls played even harder. Robbie even cheered her brother on more frequently.

"Come on, David," said Robbie. "Hussle."

Both teams were still playing hard, and shooting baskets like crazy. The game was going down to the wire. While the guys were trying to hang on to the lead, the girls tried in vain to catch up. Finally, when the score became tied at twenty, a car drove by, and Robbie distracted all of the players on the girls' team.

"Hey, your boyfriend just drove by," said Robbie.

Suddenly the girls stopped playing, and looked at the street.

"Whose?" asked one girl.

David, who had the ball, shot it. It went through the hoop on the guys' side, breaking the tie. The guys won.

"Hey, that wasn't fair," said several of the girls on the court. "You cheated!"

"You all should've been paying attention," said David.

"Way to go, David," said Robbie.

"Thank you, Robbie," said David.

Just then the guys on the court started congratulating him.

"Man, that was excellent," said one guy.

"If we hadn't had you," said another guy, "they might have beaten us."

"Well, thank you," said David.

"That was so cool, David," said a voice of a female. David then turned around, and saw his childhood friend, Lindsey, who was a college student.

"You play very well," she said.

"Thank you, Lindsey," said David. "I'm really, very surprised to see you here."

"I'm surprised, too," said Lindsey. "But I really came here to see you, because I haven't seen you in a long time."

"Well, I am doing wonderful," said David.

"I'm glad," said Lindsey. "Anyway, I came down here to see who's really powerful."

"What do you mean?" asked David.

"I mean, if a girl can really rule better than a guy," said Lindsey. "You and me, to eleven. Okay?"

"Well, okay," said David.

At that moment Lindsey and David started the game of one-on-one. They both played very, very hard, but Lindsey seemed to have the upper hand as far as making baskets. Robbie, as always, cheered David on to help him feel good about playing.

"Go, David!" she yelled.

Lindsey made eight baskets before David made his first basket. But sure enough, Lindsey had no problem whatsoever beating David eleven to six in the game of one-on-one.

"You're excellent, Lindsey," said David.

"Thank you, David," said Lindsey. "You're excellent, too."

"But you're better than me," said David.

"Then I guess girls are more powerful than guys are," said Lindsey.

"I don't know," said David, "but you are definitely more powerful than me."

Just then the six problem girls arrived at the park in the white B.M.W. They got out of the car, and headed to the basketball court.

"Well, well, well," Carla told the other five girls. "It looks like Mr. Child Abuse Victim's ruling the basketball court."

David turned around, and saw the six problem girls.

"Oh, no!" cried David. "Not again!"

"Yeah, David," said Jennifer. "It's us."

"What do you all want now?" asked David, in a state of anger.

"You're going to play us to eleven," said Brittany.

"I beg your pardon," said David.

"You heard her," said Melanie. "She didn't stutter."

Just then Lindsey, Robbie and everyone else at the park became worried.

"You're playing us to eleven," said Brittany, "and you'd better win, or else."

"Or else what?" asked David.

"Or else, you're gonna lose you car," said Latish.

David, Robbie, Lindsey, and everyone else at the park then balked at what the six problem girls were saying.

"No, Latish!" said David, in a state of anger. "I am not giving away my car to you all."

"You're playing us to eleven, David," said Leandra, in a state of anger. "And if you don't win, you don't keep your car."

"David, they're only going to humiliate you," said Robbie.

"Don't let them rip you off, David," said Lindsey.

"So, David," said Carla, "are you ready to fight for your car?"

"You all want another car?" asked David. "Go to the dealership. I'm out of here. Let's go, Robbie."

David and Robbie then headed to their car, and Carla, who was getting angry, went after David. Lindsey, Robbie, and everyone else at the park started to get scared. When David and Robbie got to their car, Carla grabbed David's arm, and turned him around.

"Hey, leave my brother alone!" yelled Robbie.

"You stay out of this!" said Carla, in a state of anger. "You'd better listen to me, David; and you'd better listen to me good. You are going to play us to eleven on that court. And if you lose, you're not going to keep your car."

"Why should I bend over backwards for you all?" screamed David, "when all you girls have done is harm me and my girlfriend!"

Carla then slapped David in the face as hard as she could, and Robbie, Lindsey, and everyone else became stunned.

"You can say whatever you want to, David," said Carla. "But you're gonna play us for your car."

"And your sister's not gonna help you," said Brittany, "unless she wants a beating, too."

Robbie then started getting scared.

"Are you threatening Robbie?" asked David.

"Hey, I think it's best that you six young ladies leave," said a guy at the park.

"Oh, we're not going anywhere," said Leandra, "and you all can't make us leave."

"You all are going to burn in hell for mistreating David and his sister!" yelled Lindsey.

"No, David and Robbie are going to burn in hell," said Brittany. "And it's gonna happen to Robbie first."

Just then David went up to Brittany and shoved her as hard as he could. As Robbie, Lindsey, and everyone else started panicking and fearing, Brittany shoved David back, and soon the two were throwing punches like crazy. Everyone was shocked to see David and Brittany in a big fight.

"David, don't let her hurt you!" screamed Robbie.

After a while, Carla and Latish broke up the fight. Latish grabbed David's arms, and held them behind his back as Carla beat, slapped, and even punched him in the face repeatedly, as hard as she could. Everyone at the park was fearing for David, as his nose and mouth started bleeding from being slapped repeatedly. When it was all over, Robbie and Lindsey started to comfort David, who was bleeding severely.

"Are you okay?" asked Lindsey.

"Lindsey, I'm gonna get some wet paper towels," said a girl at the park. "Okay?"

"Well, I need several," said Lindsey.

Meanwhile, Robbie was crying, and one of the guys that played ball with David comforted her.

"It's okay, Robbie," said the guy.

"Thank you," whispered Robbie, who was fighting back tears..

David, who was bleeding badly, was being comforted by Lindsey, a few of the guys that played ball with him, and several girls. Everyone at the park, except for the six problem girls, were standing in shock.

"David, you don't have to give your car to them," said Lindsey. "Okay?"

"They are going to pay for what they did," said David.

"Don't say that, David," said a guy. "It might hurt you even more."

"I wonder where those paper towels are?" asked a girl at the park.

"Hey, forget the paper towels," said Melanie. Everyone that was comforting David then saw Leandra coming with a razor blade.

"Hope your happy, David," said Leandra. She then walked onto the court, and slashed his right arm with the razor blade. David then screamed, everyone comforting him became even more upset, and his arm started bleeding from the cut.

"You little winch!" yelled Lindsey. "I swear to god, you all are not going to get away with this!"

"Hey, let's get out of here," said Brittany.

"I think that's a good idea," said Carla.

As the six problem girls went and got into their car, and left the park, Lindsey, and several of the basketball players at the park began carrying David to the bathroom as his arm started bleeding heavily. Robbie was frustrated because her brother was wrongly injured while trying to fight to save his car.

That Friday at school, the halls were noisy, as lots of students were flooding the halls. David, who was at his locker getting ready for choir, started thinking about what it would be like to be chosen as the prom king. Just then Keisha approached him.

"Hey, David," she said.

"Oh," thought David. "I didn't know you were behind me."

"I'm sorry," said Keisha, "did I scare you?"

"Well, a little," said David, "but I'm okay."

At that point David closed his locker.

"So, are you going to the dance tomorrow night?" asked Keisha.

"Yes," said David. "What made you think I had changed my mind?"

"Because I'm planning on meeting you there," said Keisha.

"Well, I'm still planning on going," said David.

"I'm glad," said Keisha.

Later that period, in the choir room, the choir instructor was talking to all of the members about the plans for the school-paid concert. All of the choir members were listening.

"The concert is at 7 p.m. May 19th at the Mississippi Coliseum in Jackson," said the conductor.

"And we're going to sing about four to five songs at the concert," said a choir member.

"Right," said the conductor.

Meanwhile, there was a female friend of the six problem girls that was not even enrolled at Canaby High School wandering the halls. She was sneaking around while classes were going on. However, the choir was getting ready to sing the main song for their performance.

"Okay, we need to get this song right," said the conductor.

Just then the piano player started playing and the choir started singing. But, unfortunately, the girl in the halls found the choir room. And while the choir was singing, she snuck in, unnoticed by the conductor and piano player, and started hiding behind David. David was concentrated on singing when the unnoticed girl started touching and rubbing on him. No one in the choir room was aware of her presence.

Around lunchtime, in the cafeteria, Jenny and Kerry were eating lunch and sharing a conversation.

"Isn't this going to be fun for Keisha and David?" asked Kerry.

"It should be," said Jenny. "I mean, they're going at my expense."

"And I'll bet they'll have a really great time," said Kerry. "By the way, did you say that dance was Saturday night?"

"Yes," said Jenny. "Saturday night, at the Canaby Junior High School gymnasium."

Just then David and a female student from choir walked into the cafeteria, arguing.

"Listen, I didn't touch you in there," said a female student.

"Well, someone was touching and grabbing on me," said David, in a state of anger.

"It wasn't me," she said. "You're blaming the wrong one."

Suddenly everyone in the cafeteria was wondering what was going on.

"David, what's the matter?" asked Jenny.

"He's going around accusing me of grabbing on him in choir," said the other student.

"Somebody was touching and rubbing on me," said David.

"Are you sure?" asked Kerry.

While looking at what was happening, the six problem girls began laughing.

"It's payback time, David," said Melanie.

Meanwhile, Jenny and Kerry were trying to get to the bottom of what was happening to David.

"I'm not blaming her for this," said David. "I'm just saying that it was somebody that was touching on me in choir."

"Well, who exactly was it?" asked Kerry.

"I don't know," said David, "because we were practicing for our spring concert when it happened."

"David, if someone touched you inappropriately," said Jenny, "you need to report it to the principal."

"She's right, David," said Kerry. "Whoever did that to you can't get away with it."

Meanwhile, the problem girls were steady laughing, thinking the matter was funny. And while chaos was erupting in the cafeteria, the unenrolled girl, who was still unnoticed on school grounds, was snacking at the vending machines. She had just bought a soda.

"Doesn't it feel good to be back in David's life?" she asked herself. "At least now we can go away to somewhere new, get married, raise a family, and live happily ever after. Isn't it so wonderful? Just me and my loverboy."

In the cafeteria, most of the students were trying to get to the bottom of what happened to David.

"This is not fair," said a choir member. "David's got a lot going for him, and lots of other students want to ruin it for him."

"All I'm saying is that someone went rubbing on me in choir today," said David.

Just then Courtney walked into the cafeteria.

"David, are you okay?" she asked.

"No, he isn't okay," said Jenny.

"Since you're so curious, Courtney," said Kerry, "someone went touching on him in choir this morning."

"What?" asked Courtney. "Are you sure they did that to you?"

"Yes, Courtney," said David.

Just then several administrators overheard the conversation.

"Is everything okay over here?" asked a teacher.

"There's a stranger in our school," said Courtney.

"Courtney, it's okay," said David.

"David, that's not okay," said the U.S. History teacher. "If someone touched you inappropriately, you need to report it to the principal."

"Courtney, did you say that a stranger is in our school?" asked a school counselor.

"Yes," said Courtney.

"How did he get in?" asked the counselor.

"Maybe she broke a window to get in," said a choir member.

"Or, maybe someone was foolish enough to let her in," said another choir member.

Meanwhile, Keisha was in the office talking to the principal. She was aware of the choir incident.

"I know that a stranger snuck into the choir room and went feeling and rubbing on David," said Keisha, "because I saw him squirming when we were practicing a difficult song for our concert performance in Jackson."

"Well, do you know who it was?" asked the principal.

"I'm not sure," said Keisha. "I know it was a girl that snuck in."

"Did the choir conductor see her?" asked the principal.

"I'm not sure," said Keisha, "because we were really busy practicing for the performance."

Just then they heard a knock at the door. It was a female choir member named Erica Brooks that had proof of the stranger on the school campus. The principal answered the door.

"May I help you?" asked the principal.

"Keisha is right," said Erica. "There is a stranger on the school premises. This surveillance tape proves it."

"Maybe we need to look at the tape," said Keisha.

At that moment Keisha, the principal, and Erica went into the teacher's lounge to view the tape. And sure enough, the tape showed the unenrolled girl wandering the halls, sneaking into the choir room, and bothering David.

"You two were right," said the principal. "Someone's not taking care of their responsibilities."

"I think she broke a window at the back door to get in," said Erica.

Erica then showed the principal the back doors, and sure enough, glass was all over the floor, windows in three doors were broken, and they both found bricks that the unenrolled student used to help gain entry.

"Who is this girl?" asked the principal.

"I heard she's a friend of the six girls that are giving David and Keisha trouble," said Erica. "I think her name is Denise Strong."

"Denise Strong," said the principal. "That's the girl I caught selling drugs to other students last year, and I had her expelled from here."

A while later, police officers were rushing to the school to answer to the criminal complaint that the principal had filed. It was around the noon hour when about eight police cars were on the campus. The school campus was blocked off with police tape as students, teachers and administrators were standing outside the school building.

"She's in here!" yelled the principal.

The police officers then ran inside the school building. Meanwhile, Erica showed the police the broken window and the broken glass.

"This is how she got in," she said, "by breaking this window."

"I will be," said a police officer.

Just then the unenrolled girl slipped past Erica and the police officers.

"I think that's her there," said Erica.

"Where?" asked another police officer.

The unenrolled girl started running, and the police officers quickly reacted.

"Freeze!" yelled a third police officer.

The other police officers inside the building fired their guns, and the unenrolled girl suddenly threw herself up against two lockers.

"Who are you all?" asked the unenrolled girl.

"Canaby Police," said the first police officer, "we have a warrant for your arrest."

"Turn around and get your hands up," said a fourth police officer.

Erica was witnessing the whole ordeal.

"Let's go!" shouted a fifth officer. "Get your hands up now!"

The unenrolled girl put her hands up, and sure enough, several police officers threw her to the floor. The first police officer then handcuffed her.

"You're under arrest for Breaking and Entering and Criminal Trespassing," said the first police officer. "You have the right to remain silent. Anything you say can and will be used against you in a court of law."

About a half-hour later, police were taking the unenrolled girl, who was Denise Strong, to jail. The entire campus was crowded as parents were on campus comforting their kids, and trying to find out what really happened. The principal then made an announcement.

"Listen up, everyone," he said. "Classes are canceled for the rest of the day."

While the entire school was in chaos, Keisha, David, and Laura found a lone tree on the school campus to stand under while sharing a conversation. David was frustrated because he ended up being the victim of a burglar.

"Can I just have a normal day at school?" he asked.

"What do you mean?" asked Laura.

"I mean, every time I think of Keisha," said David, "something bad happens to me."

"David, let me share a secret with you," said Keisha.

"Well, okay," said David.

"I want us to be remembered at Canaby High School as two students with dark, lonely childhoods who defied the odds and proved some experts wrong," said Keisha.

"It looks like that's going good," said David.

"That's another reason Keisha is running for prom queen, and hoping that she wins the title," said Laura. "We're also hoping that you get chosen as the prom king."

"This is really sweet of both of you," said David.

"See, I want most of the students and faculty members here at Canaby High School," said Keisha, "especially the Senior class, to see that we're right for each other."

"I see what's going on now," said David.

"I'm glad you do," said Laura.

"David, can I ask you something?" asked Keisha.

"Yes, Keisha," said David.

"After all that we've been through up to right now," said Keisha, "can you look me in the eyes and say that we really and truly deserve each other?"

"Yes, Keisha," said David.

"That's just what I wanted to hear," said Keisha.

Keisha and David then kissed each other.

"Are you ready for the junior high dance tomorrow night?" asked Laura.

"Yes," said David. "I'm ready for anything."

"Well, I'm really happy that you're looking forward to the junior high dance," said Keisha.

Would Keisha be able to actually win the prom queen title? Would David really be chosen as the prom king? The only thing that stood between Keisha, David, and the prom queen and prom king titles was the final support of the Senior class, which was bound to be good.

ELEVEN

When it was time for the Canaby Junior High School spring dance to take place, the outside of the school was crowded, as lots of teenagers were sharing conversations while waiting for the dance to start. It was a Saturday night, around seven o' clock. When Keisha and David arrived on the school premises, they headed to the gymnasium. They were both dressed up for the dance.

"I hope I have fun here," said David.

"I'm sure you will," said Keisha. "At least those six girls aren't around to bother you."

"I'm glad," said David. "Remember what we talked about yesterday afternoon?"

"About what?" asked Keisha.

"About spending some time together for once," said David.

"Yes," said Keisha. "I remember."

"If I make it through this," said David, "I gotta thank Jenny, since she was the one that invited us down here."

"That's right," said Keisha.

At the dance, there was a band that consisted of two keyboard players, three guitar players, a drum player, an electric bass player, and a tenor saxophone player, playing a fast song that most of the kids and teenagers, between the ages of eleven and eighteen, were enjoying. Refreshments, such as cookies, cake, ice cream, and fruit punch, were also being served. But when the group started to play a slow song, lots of girls started asking boys to dance with them. Sure enough, Keisha did the same thing with David. And when that happened, Keisha and David started slow-dancing to the song that was playing. After a while, lots of teenagers that were slow-dancing to the song started observing Keisha and David.

"They can really go," said a fourteen-year-old girl.

"I'll bet they're in love with each other," said the twelve-year-old boy she was dancing with.

Keisha and David continued slow-dancing.

"I haven't seen Jenny yet," said David.

"Maybe she isn't here yet," said Keisha. "But she should be here soon."

"I'm glad," said David, "because she was the one that invited us down here."

Just then Jenny arrived at the dance. And when she saw Keisha and David slow-dancing, she had a smile on her face. When the slow song was finished, Keisha and David went to the refreshment table to have some fruit punch.

"David, I can tell that you're enjoying yourself so far," said Keisha.

"How did you figure that out?" asked David.

"I've just noticed it," said Keisha.

"Hey, Keisha," said Jenny.

Keisha and David turned around, and saw Jenny.

"Hey, Jenny," said Keisha. "David just asked about you."

"Did he?" asked Jenny.

"Yes," said David. "I just hadn't seen you here."

"I'm just a little late, that's all," said Jenny. "Anyway, are you having fun so far, David?"

"Yes," said David. "I'm having a great time here."

Just then Courtney arrived at the dance.

"Hello, David," she said.

"Keisha, Jenny, it's not our fault that she's here," said David. "Let's just let her be. Okay?"

"Well, okay," said Keisha.

Just then a thirteen-year-old boy named Eric recognized Courtney at the dance.

"Hey, Courtney," he said.

Courtney turned around, and saw him.

"Hey, Eric," said Courtney. "I haven't seen you in a long time."

"I haven't seen you either," said Eric. "I didn't know you were coming down here."

"Well, I tricked you," said Courtney.

Just then the band started playing a fast song.

"Would you like to dance, Eric?" asked Courtney.

"Of course, Courtney," said Eric.

At that moment Keisha, David, and Jenny watched as Courtney and Eric danced to the song. They danced in a really crazy way. So crazy that lots of other teenagers had to form two lines. After a while mostly everyone at the dance cheered Courtney and Eric on. When the song was finished, everyone applauded for the show that Courtney and Eric put on.

"That was an excellent display, Courtney," said Jenny.

"Thank you, Jenny," said Courtney.

Just then the band started playing a slow song at the dance, and Courtney and Eric decided to slow-dance to the song. And Keisha was dancing with a fifteen-year-old boy, while Jenny was dancing with a fourteen-year-old boy. David just watched as lots of other teenagers were slow-dancing to the song. But he wasn't aware that a seventeen-year-old girl was standing by herself, too. She spotted David, and walked up to him.

"Hey," she said.

"Oh, hi," said David.

"You look like a nice young man," said the seventeen-year-old girl.

"I am," said David.

"Would you like to dance?" she asked.

"I'd love to," said David.

Just then David and the seventeen-year-old girl started dancing to the song. She put her arms around him, and he started to feel a little nervous.

"I'm not scaring you, am I?" she asked.

"No," said David. "You're not scaring me at all."

"I'm so glad," she said, "because I think you're a really nice guy for a shy girl like me to dance with."

"Well, thank you," said David. "But not everyone at Canaby High School thinks that of me."

"Do you go to Canaby High?" she asked.

"Yes," said David. "I see you almost all the time."

"Well, I never see you," she said.

"I'm David Malone," said David.

"Oh," thought the seventeen-year-old girl, "you're Keisha Blackledge's boyfriend."

"Yeah, that's me," said David.

"Then you're better off than me," said the seventeen-year-old girl.

"What do you mean?" asked David.

"I mean, I don't have a boyfriend," said the seventeen-year-old girl, "and I don't know how to get one."

"I'm sure you'll get one someday," said David. "If it happened to me, I know it'll happen to you."

"I doubt it," she said, "but thanks very much."

"It's no problem," said David. "At least we can still be best friends."

"Well, okay," she said. "I wish you and Keisha good luck, though."

"Well, thanks," said David. "What's your name?"

"Savannah Maxie," she said. "I'm eleventh grade if you're wondering."

"Then you can run for prom queen next year," said David.

"That's right," said Savannah.

When the song was finished, David and Savannah went to the refreshment table for fruit punch. Keisha was headed to the refreshment table, too.

"David, are you having fun so far?" asked Keisha.

"I'm great," said David. "I'd like you to meet someone. This is Savannah Maxie."

Keisha and Savannah then shook hands.

"David, we've met before," said Keisha. "We've had some classes together, and she's a basketball cheerleader. She's also a member of the Dream Daisies dance team."

"Well, I just didn't know," said David.

"It's okay," said Keisha.

"But he is a nice guy," said Savannah.

Just then the emcee of the Canaby Junior High School spring dance, a senior at Canaby High School, walked upon the stage.

"Thank you, everyone," she said. "This group has done a really great job performing for us here at the Canaby Junior High School spring dance. This is one of the best pop music groups in the nation, as well as the state of Mississippi. With sixteen number one hits, seven Grammy awards, four American Music Awards, and three albums that have sold over a million copies, we are very, very delighted to have them here tonight. Let's hear it for Larry McGovern and the Angels of Love."

At that moment everyone at the dance gave the emcee a round of applause, and then she kept talking.

"Now I know that there are lots of students in grades eleven and twelve at Canaby High School that are here at the Canaby Junior High School spring dance tonight," she said, "and since this is prom season for most high schools all across the nation, this spring dance really means a lot to them. At Canaby High School, there are two popular straight-A students with painful emotional scars that are up for prom queen and prom king. And those two students are here tonight, Keisha Blackledge and David Malone. And Keisha and David, this next song is dedicated to the two of you."

At that moment the emcee stepped off of the stage, and the band started playing the slow song. Mostly everyone at the dance, including Keisha and David, started slow-dancing.

"I just can't wait until prom night," said David.

"I can't either," said Keisha. "But prom night isn't far."

"I mean, it's next month," said David.

"Actually, it's three weeks from tonight," said Keisha.

"Well, I'll wait just for you," said David.

"That's so sweet," said Keisha. "Did you have fun tonight?"

"Yes, I did," said David. "I had a lot of fun."

"I'm so glad," said Keisha.

When the junior high dance was over that night, Keisha drove David home. It was around eleven o' clock.

"I really had a great time tonight," said David.

"I'm glad you did," said Keisha. "At least now we can both feel what prom night will be like."

"That's right," said David.

"David, can I ask you something?" asked Keisha.

"Yes, Keisha," said David.

"After what happened to the two of us tonight," said Keisha, "can you look me in the eyes and say that we really and truly deserve each other?"

"Yes, Keisha," said David.

"That's just what I wanted to hear," said Keisha.

Keisha and David then kissed each other. They had every reason to be happy about the senior prom, which wasn't for another three weeks. That would be the night the whole school would see them as a happy couple.

TWELVE

The very next week at school, the halls were noisy and crowded as lots of students were looking forward to prom night. It was during morning break, and David was at his locker getting his books ready for his third period class. When he closed his locker, he started heading toward the snack bar. He then saw Keisha standing across the hall with a smile on her face.

"Hey, David," she said.

"What are you up to, Keisha?" asked David.

"I thought about you the rest of the weekend," said Keisha.

"Did you?" asked David.

"Yes," said Keisha.

"That's really sweet of you," said David. "I'm going to the snack bar. Do you wanna walk there with me?"

"I'd love to," said Keisha.

While the snack bar was crowded that morning, Keisha and David were sharing a conversation while enjoying sodas and jelly doughnuts.

"Keisha, things are getting a little bit better for me," said David.

"I'm glad to hear that," said Keisha.

"I mean, you were chosen as Homecoming Queen," said David, "I was chosen as escort, we were voted class favorites, and now we're up for prom queen and prom king. Isn't that wonderful?"

"Yes, David," said Keisha. "It's very wonderful. Those are some of the good times that we've had in our memorable Senior year."

"But what about the bad times we've had this year?" asked David.

"What do you mean?" asked Keisha.

"I mean, like incidents involving those six girls that are trouble to me," said David.

"David, let's try to focus on the good times," said Keisha. "Okay?"

"Well, okay," said David.

Just then mostly everyone in the snack bar noticed Brianna and Jodi smiling and giggling while they were staring at Keisha and David.

"What's your problem?" asked Keisha.

"We're proud of David," said Brianna. "We really are."

"Yeah," said Keisha, "I figured you all would be."

"Keisha, I'm not trying to take this the wrong way," said David, "but . . ."

David then heard car keys jiggle, and looked at Brianna and Jodi. They smiled at him.

"You have pretty eyes, David," said Jodi.

"David, don't pay any attention to them," said Keisha.

"I'm trying not to," said David.

Just then Brianna and Jodi left the snack bar.

"Bye, David," said Jodi.

"David, I think that we should focus more on the good times than the bad times," said Keisha. "Do you understand?"

"Yeah, Keisha," said David, "I'm with you all the way."

David then stood up and checked his pockets, only to find his keys were missing.

"Those girls got my car keys," said David.

David then walked out of the snack bar, and Keisha followed him.

"David, where are you going?" asked Keisha.

In the hallway, which was noisy and packed, Brianna and Jodi were laughing and giggling when David, in a state of anger, found them. Brianna suddenly turned around.

"Oh, hi, David," she said. "How are you doing?"

"Give me my car keys," said David.

"We don't have your keys," said Jodi.

"You all are liars," said David. "Give me my car keys."

Just then Keisha and Courtney found David.

"David, are you okay?" asked Courtney.

"These two girls have got my car keys," said David.

"Please give David his car keys," said Courtney.

"We don't have them," said Brianna.

"Let me see your pockets," said Keisha.

Paulette's two friends then emptied their pockets, but the keys were nowhere in sight.

"I told you we didn't have them," said Brianna.

"Why don't you all just leave David alone?" suggested Courtney. "Because the last thing we want to see is him pitching a fit in front of everyone."

Just then the six problem girls came out of the teacher's lounge with sodas. Melanie had David's car keys.

"Hey David?" she asked, "it looks like you won't be driving your car for a while."

"Wait a minute," said Keisha, "what are you six girls doing in the teacher's lounge?"

"Just lounging around and having fun," said Latish.

"And how did you get David's car keys, Melanie?" asked Courtney.

"In a very, very special way," said Melanie.

"Did you two girls give my car keys to her?" David then asked Paulette's friends.

"No, we didn't," said Jodi.

"Bye, David," said Carla.

Just then the six problem girls headed to class with David's car keys.

"David, it will be okay," said Keisha.

When third period started, Courtney was comforting David in the U.S. History class. David was upset because of the loss of his car keys.

"David, I know you're upset about your car keys," said Courtney, "but you don't need to make such a big deal out of it."

"Courtney, I have got to get my keys back," said David. "I just can't go around telling my mom and dad that I lost my car keys to those girls."

Just then the bell rang, and the teacher walked in.

"Good morning, everyone," said the teacher. "I have to talk to all of you. There is speculation that those six girls that keep troubling

Keisha and David helped Denise Strong break into the school last week."

"Why do they like to trouble Keisha and David in the first place?" asked a student in the class.

"It's no telling," said Savannah. "David's got a lot of popularity, and popularity is all those girls are after."

"See, Keisha is running for prom queen," said Kerry, "and David is supporting her. Those six girls are just jealous because most of the school is happy for Keisha and David."

"You all have a point there," said the teacher. "No student has the right to make fun of Keisha and David just because of Keisha's prom queen success."

"But is that going to get my car back anytime soon?" asked David.

"Relax, David," said the teacher.

"Look, my car is important to me," said David.

"David, calm down," said Courtney.

Just then David stormed out of the classroom.

"David," said the teacher.

David was headed for the classroom where the six problem girls were, which was a ninth-grade English class, when Courtney found him.

"Hey David?" asked Courtney, "where are you going?"

"If you all aren't going to take care of this," said David, "I'll just have to take care of it myself."

"David, please don't create a scene," said Courtney.

"Courtney, I'm trying to stay as calm as I can," said David, "but I need to get my car keys back before they end up wrecking my car. Because if they wreck it, I'm going to have to pay for damages."

"David, you're going to get your car keys back before this day is over," said Courtney.

"Do you promise?" asked David.

"I promise," said Courtney.

"Thank you, Courtney," said David. "I really appreciate you helping me out."

"It's no problem," said Courtney.

At that moment Courtney gave David a big hug.

When morning break came, the six problem girls were at their lockers on the ninth-grade hall sharing a huge conversation when Latasha and Cheryl showed up. It was around ten-fifty-five, between third and fourth periods, and the hallway was noisy and crowded.

"Hey Carla?" asked Latasha, "give me David's car keys."

"We don't have David's car keys," said Carla.

"You six girls are lying," said Cheryl. "We know it."

"How do you all know?" asked Leandra.

"Courtney told us about it," said Latasha.

"She told us that Melanie had David's keys in her pocket," said Cheryl.

Latasha and Cheryl then caught the six problem girls in a lie. The problem girls then stood in shock.

Around lunchtime that day, Shanna, Erica, and several other choir members were talking about Keisha's successful run for the prom queen title. The cafeteria was serving bacon cheeseburgers and fries for lunch.

"When Keisha wears the queen's crown on prom night," said Shanna, "we should all thank her."

"Thank her for what?" asked a choir member.

"For having the courage to run," said Shanna.

"We all know how excellent of a prom queen she is going to be," said a second choir member, "but there's still the possibility that one of the fifteen underdogs could get the title."

"What do you mean by underdogs?" asked Shanna.

"I mean, one of the other fifteen girls could be wearing the prom queen's crown," said the second choir member.

"As hard as Keisha has worked for the prom queen title," said a third choir member, "there's no way she is going to lose."

"I mean, I'm happy for Keisha," said the second choir member, "and I voted for her, too, but elections don't guarantee the title."

"You know, he's right," said Erica. "The final vote for prom queen could go either way."

"Well, maybe it could," said Shanna, "but I really think that Keisha is going to get the title."

That night, on the football field, the elections for prom court were about to take place. Again, the football field was crowded, but unlike the prom queen elections, three guys and three girls could get elected. There were forty Senior students, including Latasha, running for prom court. After a while, the principal quieted the crowd down.

"Okay, may I have your attention, please?" he asked. "This year, for our prom court, we have forty candidates running. I would like for each candidate to introduce themselves to the large crowd that we have tonight."

Meanwhile, Keisha and David were just arriving at the prom court elections.

"David, I wanna thank you for believing in me with this 'prom queen' thing," said Keisha.

"That's no problem," said David. "I told you to try to follow your heart, and it could come true."

"I haven't gotten the prom queen title yet," said Keisha. "And who knows? I may not get it at all."

"I'm sure you'll get it," said David.

"How sure?" asked Keisha.

"I mean, you were the odds-on favorite in the elections," said David. "So you should get it."

"Well, thanks for believing in me, David," said Keisha.

"You're welcome, Keisha," said David.

Meanwhile, Latasha, who was prom court candidate number 18, was waiting her turn to introduce herself to the crowd when she saw Keisha and David arriving at the elections.

"Keisha and David are here," Latasha told the young man that was candidate number 17.

"Really?" he asked.

"Yes," said Latasha. "He and Keisha are walking through the gates right now."

Just then the young lady that was candidate number 16 handed the microphone to the young man that was candidate number 17, and he introduced himself.

"Hello, everyone," he said. "I'm prom court candidate number 17, Larry Farrar."

Larry then handed the microphone to Latasha, and she introduced herself.

"Hi, everyone," she said. "I'm candidate . . ."

"Hey, David's here!!" yelled a Canaby High football player, cutting Latasha off. Just then everyone at the elections noticed Keisha and David, and started applauding and cheering, while Latasha was embarrassed because she was cut off while trying to introducing herself.

"Latasha, it's okay," said Larry

"Thank you, Larry," said Latasha, in a state of anger. "Thank you very, very much."

Just then the principal went on stage.

"May I have your attention, please?" he asked. He then realized what was going on. The entire crowd was excited because Keisha and David were at the prom court elections. This is one more proof that Keisha and David are inseperable, by all means.

THIRTEEN

A week after the prom court elections, on a Saturday night, Keisha and David decided to take a trip to metro Jackson. They were sharing a conversation while walking through downtown Jackson.

"Keisha, you have really given me something to remember," said David. "Had it not been for you, I might be in some dark, lonely, and frightening place right now."

"It's okay, David," said Keisha. "My life's been rough, too. And mostly because of how those six problem girls have mistreated me all during my run for prom queen."

"But why did they have to try to get back at me?" asked David.

"David, dear, don't worry about it," said Keisha.

"I didn't do anything to them," said David.

"I know you didn't," said Keisha, "but they tried to hurt me as well."

"But the best thing is your campaign was a huge success," said David.

"That's right," said Keisha. "And you helped me make it through."

"Let's put it this way, Keisha," said David. "You did your part, and I did mine."

"So I guess this means now is the time to celebrate," said Keisha.

"Well, yes," said David, "but the big night isn't until next week."

"But at least we can practice here," said Keisha.

"Where?" asked David.

"Here," said Keisha. "Under the moon and stars, and in front of the city night lights."

The moon in the sky was high, and the stars in the sky were shining brightly. The night lights in downtown Jackson were very bright and beautiful. Keisha then looked back at David, and put a big smile on her face.

"Well, okay," said David. "I guess we don't have to wait until prom night."

"That's just what I wanted to hear," said Keisha.

Keisha then put her arms around David.

"This reminds me of Valentine's Day," said Keisha.

"It should," said David, "because we had a really great Valentine's Day two months ago."

"I know," said Keisha. "That was dinner and a movie. But this is more than dinner and a movie."

"Then this must be you and me after the prom," said David.

"Pretty much so," said Keisha.

"Now I know I can't wait until prom night," said David.

"It's next week," said Keisha. "In fact, it's a week from tonight."

"Then I've figured out something," said David.

"What's that?" asked Keisha.

"We'll be together in the Canaby High School Gymnasium at this time next week," said David.

"That's right," said Keisha.

Just then Keisha spotted a coffee shop in the heart of downtown.

"Wanna practice for the big night?" asked Keisha.

"Sure," said David.

A little while later, Keisha and David were seated at a table outside the coffee shop.

"I wish prom night came every year," said David.

"So do I," said Keisha. "But prom only comes once in your lifetime. And this is our time."

"That's right," said David. "This is our time."

"And I'm going to be this beautiful girl with a dark and lonely childhood past," said Keisha, "who stands to be wearing the queen's crown."

"That's right," said David.

"And everyone in the Senior class is going to be cheering us on," said Keisha.

"But what if they don't choose me as the prom king?" asked David.

"I'm sure they're going to choose you," said Keisha. "Do you remember what I told you earlier?"

"Yes, I do," said David.

"When we graduate from high school, I want us to be remembered as two bright students who fought the odds when they were against us," said Keisha. "And that's what will happen on graduation night. Do you understand?"

"Yes, I do," said David.

"So why don't we enjoy it while we can?" suggested Keisha.

"Sounds great," said David.

Just then a romantic slow song started playing through the speakers at the coffee shop.

"Let's practice for prom night," said Keisha.

"Okay," said David.

Just then Keisha and David got up from the table, and began slow-dancing to the song. She put her arms around him. After a while, a patron in the downtown area stopped in her tracks and started staring at Keisha and David while they were still dancing to the song.

"Are you okay, David?" asked Keisha.

"Yes, Keisha," said David. "I'm fine."

"I just hope I'm not scaring you," said Keisha.

"I'm okay," said David. "I promise."

"Well, I'm glad you're okay," said Keisha.

"Keisha, you never make me nervous," said David.

"Well, okay," said Keisha.

Keisha then started touching David's face, while the patron was still looking at them.

"I don't think I can wait until the big night, either," said Keisha.

At that moment Keisha and David kissed each other. While kissing, Keisha lightly touched David's right cheek and jaw. The kiss was so long that the patron started to hurry away. Keisha was so into kissing David that she even raised her left foot up. After a while, they stopped kissing.

"David, can I ask you something?" asked Keisha. Her arms were still around David.

"Sure," said David.

"Do you think following my heart will also get us married?" asked Keisha.

"Yes, Keisha," said David. "Especially after you've given me something to believe in."

"Thank you, David," said Keisha. "That's just what I wanted to hear."

Around eleven o' clock that night, at Keisha's house in Canaby, Keisha and David were spending the night together, since her mother was out of town. David's parents were away for the remainder of the night, too. That meant that Robbie was at Keisha's house, too. Keisha and David were in the den of the house trying to settle down, and Keisha had just made a fireplace. They were also sipping sparkling grape drink in wine glasses.

"Are you okay, David?" asked Keisha.

"Yes," said David. "I'm wonderfully okay."

"I am so glad another grueling week's over with," said Keisha.

"Yeah, me too," said David.

"You know what, David?" asked Keisha.

"What?" asked David.

"It's been more peaceful at Canaby High School since those six problem girls left," said Keisha.

"I'm glad," said David. "At least now I can truthfully say that I'm relieved from them."

"Now we don't have to say they stopped us from succeeding in high school," said Keisha.

"That's right," said Keisha. "They can't hinder me anymore."

"Me, either," said Keisha. "When they threatened you in the hallway that morning, that was the last time."

"And I am glad," said David.

"Me, too," said Keisha.

Meanwhile, Robbie was in Keisha's room looking through a magazine when Keisha checked up on her.

"Robbie, are you okay?" asked Keisha.

"Yes," said Robbie. "Where's mom and dad?"

"They had to go to a wedding in Sulphur, Louisiana," said Keisha, "but they'll be back here tomorrow."

"Do I have to spend the night here?" asked Robbie.

"Robbie, you'll be okay with us," said Keisha. "I promise."

"Well, okay," said Robbie.

"Robbie, if you need to see me or David," said Keisha, "we're in the back bedroom. Okay?"

"Well, okay," said Robbie.

"Good night, Robbie," said Keisha.

"Good night, Keisha," said Robbie.

When Keisha walked into the back bedroom, she saw David lying down on the bed. He was very worn out from the long night.

"Well, what do you think of the bedroom, David?" asked Keisha.

"It's great," said David.

"I know you're tired, David," said Keisha. "I'm kind of tired myself."

"I am," said David. "It's been a really rough day."

Just then Keisha climbed onto the bed.

"David, do you think we should spend the night like this on prom night?" asked Keisha.

"That's a great idea," said David.

"I mean, first, we have a special dinner," said Keisha, "then we go to the prom, then we go the the special after-prom party. Doesn't that sound great?"

"Yes, Keisha," said David. "That sounds very great."

"I just can't wait until prom night," said Keisha.

"Me, either," said David.

"And wait until we graduate as Valedictorian and Salutatorian," said Keisha.

"Oh, that I don't think will happen," said David.

"But it could by surprise," said Keisha.

"You're right," said David. "Maybe it could happen. But let's focus on prom night while we've got the chance."

"Well, okay," said Keisha.

Just then Keisha started lying down by David's side.

"David, I'm glad prom night is a week from tonight," said Keisha.

"Me, too," said David.

A while later Keisha and David went to bed. Later that night, the moon in the sky was shining brightly. And while Keisha, David, and Robbie were fast asleep, a breeze started blowing through the sky, and the night lights all over metro Jackson looked very bright and beautiful.

The next week at school, most of the students were looking forward to prom night. It was a Monday morning, just before second period, and David was at his locker getting ready for choir when Jenny approached him.

"Hi, David," she said.

"Oh, hi, Jenny," said David. "I am so glad those six girls are no longer around."

"Me, too," said Jenny. "After all you and Keisha have been through trying to get ready for the prom Saturday night, I am just about ready to see you two wear the king and queen crowns."

"Thanks, Jenny," said Keisha.

At that point David closed his locker.

"Jenny, wish me and Keisha good luck on prom night," said David.

"Well, good luck," said Jenny.

"Thank you," said David.

Later in the choir room, David, Keisha, Shanna, Kerry, and the rest of the choir members were singing the main song for the concert in Jackson. They were singing the song very well, but the conductor still heard a mistake in the song. When he did, he stopped everyone from singing.

"Stop the song," he said. "That was good, but you all have got to keep the rhythm flowing in the right direction, and you all have got to remember the right words. Let's try it again and see if we can get it completely right."

At that moment the piano player started playing the song, and then the choir began singing the song. They sang according to the rhythm, and they got the words exactly right. After a while, the song was completely finished.

"That was better," said the conductor. "Much, much better."

When that period was over, the snack bar on campus was open, since it was during morning break. The snack bar was crowded, and most of the tables were filled as lots of students were enjoying snacks. David was headed to the snack bar to buy his morning break favorite: jelly doughtnuts and a soda, and Keisha was by his side. But when David and Keisha got to the snack bar, the line to the window was long.

"Oh, boy," said David. "This is the last thing we need."

"David, it will be okay," said Keisha. "Besides, class doesn't start until ten-fifteen."

"Well, okay," said David.

At ten o' clock, Keisha and David were seated, and enjoying jelly doughnuts and sodas. They had just been served, and the line to the window was broken down. But the snack bar was still fairly crowded.

"See, David," said Keisha. "I told you that we would be served before long."

"That's only because some other students chose to leave," said David.

"Well, they're the ones missing out on the snack bar," said Keisha.

"That's right," said David. "They're only giving up their chance to buy snacks."

"Anyway, I need to ask you something," said Keisha.

"What's that?" asked David.

"After what's happened between us in the last few weeks, like the junior high dance, and spending last Saturday night together," said Keisha, "can you look me in the eyes and say that we really and truly deserve each other?"

"Yes, I can," said David.

"That's just what I wanted to hear," said Keisha.

At that moment Keisha and David kissed each other, in front of everyone in the snack bar. The other students started wowing Keisha and David.

"Wouldn't it be great if they married each other this coming summer?" asked a girl at the snack bar.

"David, she's probably right," said Keisha.

"What do you mean?" asked David.

"We probably should get married sometime this summer," said Keisha.

When the day of the senior prom came, David and Keisha were so thrilled to death. While David was at his house getting ready for the big night, he happened to be thinking about Keisha. And while Keisha was at her house getting ready for the big night, she happened to be thinking about David. David was planning to wear a black tuxedo to the prom, while Keisha was planning to wear a white formal dress to the prom. Soon David had his tuxedo on, and when he did, his sister, Robbie, saw him.

"Wow, David," said Robbie. "You look handsome."

"Thanks, Robbie," said David. "Can I ask you something?"

"Yes, you can, David," said Robbie.

"Do you think Keisha will like this tuxedo?" asked David.

"I'm sure she will," said David.

Just then David's mom and dad saw him in his tuxedo.

"You look handsome, David," said his father.

"Thanks, dad," said David.

"You look very, very handsome, David," said his mother. "Just wait until Keisha sees you in that tuxedo."

"That's what I'm hoping for," said David.

"I'm sure she'll adore you in that tuxedo," said Robbie.

"She'll probably be thrilled to see you in it," said his mother.

"Well, I won't know until she sees me," said David.

"Trust me, David," said his father, "she'll like you in that tuxedo."

Meanwhile, Keisha was ready for the senior prom, too. She had on her white formal dress, and her mother took a look at Keisha.

"Keisha, you look very, very beautiful," said her mother.

"Thanks, mom," said Keisha. "Can I ask you something?"

"You sure can," said her mother.

"Do you think David will like this dress?" asked Keisha.

"I'm sure he will," said her mother.

"Thanks, mom," said Keisha. "That's just what I wanted to hear."

At that moment Keisha gave her mother a big hug.

"I'm proud of you, Keisha," said her mother.

"Thanks," said Keisha. "You're the best mother in the world." Around seven o' clock that Saturday night, the senior prom at Canaby High School, which was to be held in the gymnasium, was about to begin. Lots of twelfth-grade students were gathered outside the Canaby High School gymnasium when Keisha and David arrived in her car. When they got out of the car, Keisha and David started walking toward the gymnasium together.

"I really like your tuxedo, David," said Keisha.

"Thank you, Keisha," said David. "You look very beautiful yourself."

"David, did you know that I really enjoy dating you?" asked Keisha.

"No," said David. "I didn't know that."

"I mean, I'm really thrilled to be going to my senior prom with a guy that I really want to spend the rest of my life with," said Keisha.

"Keisha, you just don't know how special that makes me feel," said David.

"Why don't we talk about it on the dance floor?" suggested Keisha. "Okay?"

"Well, okay," said David.

When the senior prom started, the band that was performing started singing a fast song, and most of the 328 seniors that were at the prom, including Keisha and David, were dancing to the song. Most of the administrators and faculty members at the prom were pleased with the turnout. The gymnasium was all decorated with ribbons and balloons, and there was a big poster on the gym stage that read, "Senior Prom." Refreshments, such as cookies, cake, ice cream, and fruit punch, were also being served at the prom.

"This is most likely the best turnout we've ever had," said the principal.

"That's right," said the assistant principal. "Over 300 students are here for this year's prom."

"And I heard that this is a very special prom," said the secretary.

"It is," said the principal. "Because I've got a surprise for all the students."

"What's the surprise?" asked the secretary.

"You all will just have to wait and see," said the principal.

Later at the prom, the music group started to perform a slow song, and while Keisha wanted to dance with a football player, Savannah Maxie wanted to dance with David.

"David, is it okay if I dance with him?" asked Keisha, referring to the football player that was by her side.

"That's perfectly okay with me," said David.

"Thank you," said Keisha.

Just then Savannah found David.

"Hey David?" she asked, "would you like to dance with me?"

"Of course, Savannah," said David.

Meanwhile, Keisha and the football player were sharing a conversation while dancing.

"So, which college are you going to?" asked Keisha.

"Probably Florida State," said the football player, "because they have one of the best football programs in the country."

"I heard they have a wonderful football team," said Keisha.

"They do," he said. "In fact, I toured the campus earlier this year, and met the football coach there."

"That's wonderful," said Keisha. "Very, very wonderful."

"Do you think I'll get a scholarship to go there?" asked the football player.

"I don't know," said Keisha. "Do you really wanna go there?"

"Well, yes," he said. "I'm planning on playing football there in the fall, and there have been talks about my being recruited to play football at Florida State."

"Well, good luck," said Keisha. "I hope it goes good."

Meanwhile, Savannah was also sharing a conversation while dancing with David.

"So, which college are you going to after you graduate?" asked Savannah.

"Probably Canaby Junior College," said David.

"Really?" asked Savannah.

"Yes," said David. "I mean, I'm just not into going far away like everyone else."

"Then maybe we can have some classes together at CJC," said Savannah.

"We could," said David. "I just don't know what I'm taking there yet."

"But we'll still see each other," said Savannah.

"That's right," said David.

"David, if you come to football and basketball games at CJC," said Savannah, "you'll get to see me cheer."

"That's right," said David. "But you've got another year to go."

"I was talking about the fall of 1997," said Savannah.

"I'll just have to see what happens," said David.

"But at least you can see me cheer at Canaby High School basketball games and see me perform with the Dream Daisies at Canaby High School football games next year," said Savannah.

"I plan to do just that anyway," said David.

"Well, I'll be looking for you," said Savannah.

"And I'll be looking for you at CJC in the fall of 1997," said

"That's so sweet of you, David," said Savannah.

What would David's life be like after high school? What would college be like for David? Would he still be able to remember his friends from high school long after graduation? And would he be able to spend the rest of his life with Keisha? Only the big night and his high school graduation stood between him and his fate for the future.

FOURTEEN

Later that night, the moon in the sky was shining brightly, and the stars in the sky looked very bright and beautiful. As for the senior prom, the band was playing a slow song, and most of the students were slow-dancing to the song. David was dancing with Courtney, and they were sharing a conversation.

"David, aren't you glad graduation day is near?" asked Courtney.

"Yes," said David. "I just can't wait to graduate."

"Which college are you thinking about going to?" asked Courtney.

"Probably Canaby Junior College," said David.

"You mean, you aren't going to State, or Ole Miss?" asked Courtney, "or even Harvard or Yale?"

"I could," said David, "but I just don't feel like leaving this area right now."

"Well, whichever college or university you decide on," said Courtney, "please let me know."

"But it will probably be when I graduate from CJC before I start thinking about a four-year school," said David.

"But at least we can have some classes together at Canaby Junior College," said Courtney.

"Yeah, Courtney," said David. "Maybe so."

When that slow song was over, the principal walked onto the stage to announce the Prom Court. David was standing by Courtney when Keisha found him.

"I hope all of you seniors that are about to graduate from Canaby High School next month are enjoying this year's Senior Prom," said the principal.

Just then Keisha found David.

"David, are you okay?" asked Keisha.

"Yes," said David. "I'm fine."

"He's wonderfully okay, Keisha," said Courtney.

"Well, thanks for taking care of him, Courtney," said Keisha.

Meanwhile, the principal announced the Prom Court.

"At this time, I would like to announce this year's Prom Court," said the principal.

Everyone in the gym then gave the principal a round of applause.

"For this year's Prom Court," said the principal, "on the male side are: Brian Lindsey, Jason Foley, and Larry Farrar. You three guys come on up here."

Just then the three guys walked up on stage. They were to the principal's left.

"Let's give these young men a round of applause," said the principal.

Just then the crowd gave the three guys a round of applause.

"Now, on the female side of this year's Court," continued the principal, "are: Kelly Broussard, Tori Rainer, and Latasha Wayne. You three ladies come on up here."

Just then Latasha and the other two girls walked up on stage. They were to the principal's right.

"Let's give these young ladies a round of applause," said the principal.

Just then the crowd gave the three girls a round of applause.

"Now our Prom King and Prom Queen are why this year's senior prom is very special. Because, as children, these two remarkable students were abused and beaten, both physically and sexually, and they've been in and out of foster homes. But they have turned all that around, because they are straight-A students, in several school clubs, and most of the student body here at Canaby High School is happy for them. Our Prom King for this year is David Malone."

Just then David walked up on stage, and the crowd gave him a round of applause. The crown bearer on stage placed the crown on his head.

"Okay," said the principal, "our Prom Queen for this year, everyone here at Canaby High School knows really well. And she's David's girlfriend. We are very happy to have her as our 1996 Queen. She's Keisha Sheree Blackledge."

Just then everyone in the gymnasium gave Keisha a huge round of applause. Keisha then walked up on stage, and the crown bearer crowned her. An eleven-year-old girl on stage gave Keisha a dozen roses while the crowd was still applauding. Keisha was standing by David when lots of photographers at the prom began taking pictures of Keisha and David. Mostly everyone at the senior prom was thrilled to see Keisha and David posing as a happy couple, since Keisha was smiling while most of the pictures were being taken. When the photographers were finished taking pictures, and everyone stopped applauding, Keisha and David had their first dance as Queen and King.

"At this time," said the principal, "the Prom King, and Prom Queen, will have their first dance."

At that moment the band started playing a slow song at the prom, and Keisha and David walked off stage, and onto the dance floor. Everyone was happy to see Keisha and David as Prom Queen and Prom King. When Keisha and David started slow-dancing to the song, they started sharing a conversation.

"Aren't you glad we practiced?" asked Keisha.

"Yes, I am," said David. "But I still didn't expect to be the Prom King."

"Well, they surprised you," said Keisha.

"Now I've really got something to remember," said David.

"That's right," said Keisha. "But wait until after the prom tonight, and you'll have even more to remember."

"What do you mean?" asked David.

"I mean, after I give you my surprise," said Keisha, "you'll have even more to remember."

"Oh, I see," said David. "First, they surprise me with the King's crown, and then you surprise me."

"That's right," said Keisha.

"I can handle that," said David.

"By the way," said Keisha, "I'm even prouder of me than I am of you."

"Why?" asked David.

"Because my thinking proved correctly," said Keisha.

"What do you mean?" asked David.

"I mean, when I ran for Prom Queen, I was hoping to be this beautiful girl with a dark and lonely childhood," said Keisha, "that's wearing the Queen's crown. And look what's happening tonight."

"That's great, Keisha," said David.

"It is," said Keisha. "I'm this beautiful girl with a dark and lonely childhood that's wearing the Queen's crown."

"Then I guess that makes me even prouder of me," said David, "than I am of you."

"Why?" asked Keisha.

"Because my thinking proved correctly," said David.

"What do you mean?" asked Keisha.

"I mean, when I told you to try to follow your heart," said David, "and it could all work out. And look what's happening tonight."

"That's great, David," said Keisha.

"It is," said David. "Following your heart really paid off in this prom thing."

"David, maybe we should both be proud of each other at the same time," said Keisha. "Don't you think so?"

"Yes, Keisha," said David. "In fact, I see it that way right now."

"That's excellent, David," said Keisha. "That's just what I wanted to hear."

"Thank you, Keisha," said David.

When the senior prom was over that night, the outside of the school campus was noisy, as thousands of students, parents, and faculty members were congratulating the participants of the senior prom. Keisha and David, however, were on the porch to the front door of the school. It was around nine-thirty at night.

"David, I can tell you had fun in there," said Keisha.

"I did, Keisha," said David. "I had a lot of fun in there."

"I'm glad you did, David," said Keisha.

Just then a limousine arrived on the Canaby High School campus.

Mostly everyone on the school campus was wondering what was going on.

"I will be," said a Canaby High School freshman.

Meanwhile, Keisha and David were thrilled.

"There's the limo," said Keisha. "Are you ready, David?"

"I'm ready for anything, Keisha," said David.

Just then a limo chaffeur opened the door to the limo, and Keisha and David got into the limousine. Everyone on the school campus, including faculty members and administrators, were wondering what was up. The limousine then left the school premises.

"Where is that limousine taking Keisha and David?" asked the principal.

"I have no idea," said the secretary.

Later that night, at the prom night party at Jenny's house in Canaby, most of the seniors that were attending the party, such as Jenny, Kerry, and Courtney, were worried about Keisha and David not being at the party, since it was being given just for them. Music was being played, and refreshments were being served at the party.

"I can't believe we're throwing this senior prom party," said Jenny, "and Keisha and David aren't here."

"Maybe something came up," said Kerry, "and they had to go somewhere."

"Or maybe they decided to do something else to celebrate prom night," said Courtney.

"But they could have at least told us," said Jenny.

Just then Rosalynn showed up at the party.

"Hey, everyone," said Rosalynn.

"Rosalynn, what brought you here?" asked Jenny.

"I just decided to come," said Rosalynn.

"Well, we're glad you're here," said Kerry.

"I'm glad, too," said Rosalynn. "But I'm sorry that Keisha and David aren't at the party."

"Do you know why they're not here?" asked Courtney.

"Of course I do," said Rosalynn. "They're on a special cruise ship on the Mississippi River."

"You mean, you paid for Keisha and David to go on a cruise?" asked Kerry.

"I sure did," said Rosalynn.

"It's no wonder they're not here at the prom night party," said Jenny.

"But thanks for at least letting us know," said Kerry.

"When will they be back?" asked Jenny.

"Around midnight tomorrow night," said Rosalynn.

"Well, I hope they're enjoying themselves," said Courtney.

"I'm sure they are," said Rosalynn.

Around twelve-fifteen that night, Keisha and David were enjoying a romantic cruise on the Mississippi River. On the boat, they were seated at a table sharing a conversation.

"Keisha, this is the best surprise I've ever had," said David.

"I told you that you were going to like it, David," said Keisha.

"At least now we have time alone," said David.

"That's right," said Keisha. "No one is around to make fun of us, or humiliate us."

"Keisha, what are our classmates doing at the prom night party?" asked David.

"I don't know," said Keisha. "But this is better than the prom night party. Don't you think?"

"Well, yes," said David. "I mean, you had a surprise for me, and I really like it. Very, very much."

"I'm glad you do, David," said Keisha.

Just then a cocktail waitress on the cruise line went to the table where Keisha and David were sitting at.

"Is everything okay over here?" asked the waitress.

"Yes," said Keisha. "We're just fine."

"Aren't you two David Malone and Keisha Blackledge?" asked the waitress.

"Yes," said David. "That's us."

"I knew it," said the waitress. "I knew there was a romantic high school couple on this boat whose trip was paid for by a college student."

"That's right," said Keisha. "We're very romantic."

"I'm so glad," said the waitress. "I have a surprise for the two of you. Okay?"

"Well, okay," said Keisha.

Just then the waitress went to get the surprise.

"David, aren't you glad we chose this cruise instead of the prom night party?" asked Keisha.

"Yes, Keisha," said David. "I'm so glad."

Just then the waitress came out with two wine glasses, and a bottle of sparkling champagne in a jar of ice."

"Here you go," said the waitress. "Sparkling champagne for the two of you."

"Ooohh, thank you very much," said a nervous, excitable Keisha."

"You didn't have to do this," said David. "You really didn't."

"But I want your romantic cruise to be even more special," said the waitress.

"Oh," thought David. "We see what's going on now."

"If you need me," said the waitress, "I'm in the kitchen. "Okay?" she then asked.

"Okay," said Keisha.

At that moment the waitress went back into the kitchen, and Keisha and David continued their conversation while enjoying the champagne.

"First, the Senior Prom," said Keisha, "and then a romantic cruise on the Mississippi River. Isn't this enough to call a special prom night?"

"Yes," said David. "This is a great way to remember the big night."

At that moment they saw the moon in the sky.

"Keisha, I see the moon shining up there," said David.

"Where?" asked Keisha.

"Over there," said David.

Suddenly Keisha and David got up from the table, and went toward the right edge of the boat to see the moon. While the moon looked very pretty to them, they also saw city lights.

"David, I've just figured out something," said Keisha.

"What's that?" asked David.

"We're getting closer to Vicksburg," said Keisha.

"You're right, Keisha," said David.

At that point Keisha and David moved away from the edge of the boat.

"David, you really mean a lot to me," said Keisha.

"Thanks, Keisha," said David. "You mean a lot to me, too."

"I'm so glad," said Keisha. "When we met each other in the ninth grade at Canaby High School, we were both faced with depression and abuse."

"I know," said David. "That's something that I don't ever want to bring up again."

"You know, David, the odds were against us then," said Keisha. "Nobody expected either one of us to make it through high school. But look what Canaby High School has done for us."

"We proved the odds wrong," said David.

"That's right," said Keisha. "We're both straight-A students, we're both very popular at Canaby High School, we're both in several school clubs, and now we're the Queen and King of our Senior Prom. Isn't that wonderful?"

"Yes," said David. "That's very, very wonderful."

"But what if we actually did end up as Valedictorian and Salutatorian?" asked Keisha.

"It will be wonderful," said David. "Really wonderful."

Just then the boat reached the city of Vicksburg, and Keisha and David saw the city lights, as well as casino lights, shining brightly. Soon, they saw the Mississippi River bridge. Lots of cars and trucks from Interstate 20 were passing on the bridge.

"I guess we'll really remember the night now," said Keisha.

Suddenly a love song began to play on the boat.

"Would you like to dance, David?" asked Keisha.

"Yes, Keisha," said David. "I'd love to."

Just then Keisha and David started slow-dancing to the song. Soon, the cocktail waitress saw Keisha and David dancing to the song.

"Isn't that sweet?" asked the waitress. "They really and truly love each other."

While Keisha and David were still slow-dancing to the song, the boat went under the Interstate 20 bridge. Soon, the lights of downtown Vicksburg could be seen. The song was almost over.

"Can I ask you something, David?" asked Keisha.

"Yes, you can, Keisha," said David.

"After all that we've experienced tonight, including me being chosen as the prom queen and you as the prom king," said Keisha, "can you look me in the eyes and say that we really and truly deserve each other?"

"Yes, I can, Keisha," said David.

"That's just what I wanted to hear," said Keisha.

At that moment Keisha put her arms around David, and kissed him, in front of the waitress, as well as the downtown lights. While they were kissing, Keisha lightly touched David's cheek, and raised her left foot up. The waitress was nervous to see Keisha and David kissing.

"That's so sweet," said the waitress. "I'll bet they're going to marry each other someday."

Keisha and David were still kissing as the boat was passing by the downtown lights. By what was happening to Keisha and David, anyone could see that they make a very excellent couple.

FIFTEEN

When it got closer to graduation time, Keisha, David, Jenny, Kerry, Courtney, Latasha, Cheryl, Ronnie, Shanna, and Erica were all gathered in the snack bar. Keisha and David were talking about what happened to them that night in the hours after the prom. It was during morning break, around nine-fifty in the morning, and the snack bar was crowded.

"David, you didn't tell us you and David were going on a cruise on prom night," said Jenny.

"Well, we didn't know, either," said Keisha.

"But Keisha had a surprise for me," said David, "and that was the surprise."

"Well, did you all like it?" asked Kerry.

"Yes, we did," said Keisha. "We went down the Mississippi River from Natchez to Helena, Arkansas."

"And Rosalynn paid for it," said Courtney.

"That's right," said David.

"Well, we're glad you all liked the special cruise better than the prom night party," said Courtney.

"We're still happy for Keisha and David," said Latasha, "even though they weren't at the prom night party."

"You know, Keisha and David are setting a wonderful example for the Freshman and Sophomore classes," said Cheryl.

"Keisha, how yould you feel if you were chosen as class Valedictorian?" asked Courtney.

"I'd be thrilled," said Keisha, "really thrilled."

"And David, how would you feel if you ended up as class Salutatorian?" asked Shanna.

"I'd probably be thrilled, too," said David.

"How do you all know Keisha and David are going to be Valedictorian and Salutatorian?" asked Ronnie.

"See, they've got highest honors," said Courtney. "They're both straight-A students, in several school clubs, and very, very popular here at Canaby High School."

"And wouldn't that be great?" asked Erica.

"Wouldn't what be great?" asked Shanna.

"To see the Prom Queen and Prom King as Valedictorian and Salutatorian," said Erica.

"That would be really, really great," said Keisha.

Just then the bell rang, meaning it was time for third period.

"Well, there's the class bell," said Courtney.

"Time for third period," said Erica.

Just then everyone in the snack bar started clearing out, and heading for class. The halls became crowded, and Jenny, Keisha, David, and Courtney were together as they left the snack bar.

"Jenny, I would like for you and Keisha to save seats for me and Courtney in the cafeteria," said David.

"Don't worry, David," said Jenny. "We'll have seats saved for you and Courtney."

"Thanks Jenny," said David.

David then kissed Keisha on the cheek.

"I'll see you at lunchtime, David," said Keisha.

"I'll see you then, too," said David. "Bye, Keisha."

"Bye, David," said Keisha.

David and Courtney then headed to the U.S. History class, sharing a conversation at the same time.

"So, are you about ready for school to be over?" asked Courtney.

"Yes," said David. "I can't wait."

"Are you ready to tour the Canaby Junior College campus next week?" asked Courtney.

"Yes," said David. "I'm thrilled about it."

"Me, too," said Courtney. "I just can't wait to tour the campus."

David and Courtney then made it to the U.S. History class.

"Better yet, we might be able to tour the campus together," said Courtney.

"That's right," said David.

Just then the bell rang, and the teacher walked in.

"Good morning, everyone," said the teacher. "Today, I am going to start getting you all ready for the final exam. I'm also going to tell you how your final grade in here will be determined. We've had six homework assignmemts, five class assignments, and thirteen tests for a total of twenty-four grades."

Just then David raised his hand.

"Yes, David," said the teacher.

"Will how we do on this test result in whether we get to graduate?" he asked.

"Yes, it will," said the teacher. "Some of you need to really do good on this final exam. But you're okay, David. You have a ninety-five average so far."

Just then the teacher picked up a list of students that were exempt from final exams off her desk. David and Courtney were on that list.

"As a matter of fact, David," said the teacher, "you and Courtney are excused."

Later that period, in the library, Courtney and David were sharing a conversation.

"Aren't you happy, David?" asked Courtney. "We don't have to take final exams."

"Yes, Courtney," said David. "I'm very happy about it."

"At least now we can look forward to graduation," said Courtney, "and then going to Canaby Junior College."

"I think we're going to be touring the campus next week," said David.

"That's right, David," said Courtney. "We are supposed to tour the campus next week, because High School Day at Canaby Junior College is next week."

"And I think they're supposed to tell you if you made the dance team at Canaby Junior College next week," said David.

"Oh, I'm sure I made the dance team," said Courtney.

Just then Cheryl walked into the library.

"What are you two doing in here, Courtney?" she asked.

"We're just talking," said Courtney.

"In case you didn't know," said David, "we're exempt from final exams."

"Me, too," said Cheryl. "I can't wait for school to be over."

"I'll bet that Keisha is exempt from finals, too," said Courtney.

"I'm sure she is," said David.

"Now we can focus on graduation and college," said Cheryl.

"That's right, Cheryl," said David. "Courtney and I are going to the same college."

"He's right," said Courtney. "We're both going to Canaby Junior College in the fall."

"Well, I wish you all good luck," said Cheryl.

"Thank you," said Courtney.

"I'll just leave you two alone now," said Cheryl. "Bye."

"Bye, Cheryl," said Courtney.

At that moment Cheryl left the library, and David and Courtney carried on with their conversation.

Around lunchtime that day, Keisha, David, Jenny, Kerry, and Courtney were sharing a huge conversation while enjoying lunch.

"So, which college are you going to, Keisha?" asked Courtney.

"To the University of Alabama in Birmingham," said Keisha.

"David, while you and me root for the Braves," said Courtney, "she'll be rooting for the Crimson Tide."

"What do you mean by that?" asked Keisha.

"The Braves are the name of Canaby Junior College's football team," said Courtney.

"Courtney, what makes you think that football is the most important part of college?" asked Kerry.

"I'm just saying that college football games help establish your alma-mater," said Courtney.

"Well, what makes you think that Canaby Junior College is good enough to be David's alma-mater?" asked Keisha.

"Keisha, it's just where I want to go to school at," said David.

"David, you don't have to go there because of Courtney's dance scholarship," said Jenny.

"I'm not going there for her dance scholarship," said David.

"David, if you want to go to Canaby Junior College, that's okay," said Kerry.

"All we're saying is don't let Courtney influence you with her dance scholarship," said Jenny.

"Well, I wish Keisha good luck," said David.

"Thank you, David," said Keisha. "I wish you good luck, too, David."

"Thank you, Keisha," said David.

Later that afternoon, at David's house, Robbie was in the living room watching television when David got home. It was around three-fifteen in the afternoon.

"Hey, David," said Robbie. "How are you doing?"

"Robbie, I didn't know you were here already," said David.

"I got out of school early today," said Robbie.

"Well, school just let out for me," said David. "And so, I'm safe at home."

"Anyway, how was your cruise on the Mississippi River?" said Robbie.

"What?" asked David, in a state of concern.

"Did you enjoy your cruise?" asked Robbie.

"How did you know I went on a cruise?" asked David.

"A classmate of mine told me," said Robbie.

"I thought so, Robbie," said David. "I believe someone at your school is talking about me and Keisha."

"David, it's all over the school," said Robbie.

"What?" asked David.

"Lots of girls at my school are talking about it," said Robbie.

Just then the doorbell rang, and Robbie answered it. It was Courtney.

"Is David here?" asked Courtney.

"He's right here," said Robbie.

"David, I've found out what day next week we can tour the campus," said Courtney.

"When?" asked David.

"Tuesday of next week," said Courtney.

The following Tuesday, on the campus of Canaby Junior College, Courtney and David, accompanied by tour guides, were touring the campus along with lots of other high school students. Canaby Junior College was having a special High School Day assembly. All of the high school students were accompanied by tour guides. David and Courtney toured numerous buildings on campus, including the Student Union, Library, Humanities Building, Science Center, Mathematics Building, Fine Arts Building, History Center, Baptist Student Union, and Gameroom.

Around ten o' clock that morning, the outside of the campus was crowded as hundreds of junior college students were enjoying the break. Thousands of high school seniors that were there for high school day were also enjoying the break. At the soda machine box, Rosalynn and her friends were enjoying sodas when they spotted David and Courtney.

"Isn't that David over there?" asked a football player.

"I believe so," said a girl in the group.

"I didn't know David was here," said Rosalynn.

"Me, either," said a friend of Rosalynn.

"Hey David? Courtney?" yelled another friend of Rosalynn.

David and Courtney then noticed Rosalynn, and ran over to the soda machine box to talk to them.

"Hey David?" said Rosalynn. "What brought you and Courtney down here?"

"We're here for high school day," said David.

"And we're enjoying it so far," said Courtney.

"Well, let me introduce you to some of my friends," said Rosalynn.

Meanwhile, their tour guides were watching.

"I think they're going to like it here," said Courtney's tour guide. "Don't you think so?"

"Yes," said David's tour guide. "David and Rosalynn are childhood friends, and he and Courtney are very best friends, so they're going to fit in perfectly."

Meanwhile, David and Courtney were getting to know Rosalynn's friends.

"So are you and David going to the special High School Day assembly today?" asked Rosalynn.

"When does it start?" asked Courtney.

"At eleven o' clock, in front of the Student Union," said a softball player.

"We're probably going to be there," said David.

"Besides, I have to find out if I made the dance team," said Courtney.

"We hope you make the dance team," said Rosalynn.

"Thank you, Rosalynn," said Courtney.

"Because then we'll have another reason to go to football and basketball games," said a boy in the group.

"That's right," said another football player in the group. "We'll see Courtney perform."

"Good luck, Courtney," said another friend of Rosalynn.

"Thank you," said Courtney.

Around eleven o clock that morning, in front of the Student Union on the Canaby Junior High campus, the special High School Day assembly was taking place, as thousands of high school students from all over mid-Mississippi, as well as the Jackson area, were gathered for the special event. Some high school students were visiting booths for several college activities and organizations. Refreshments were being served, and live entertainment from the school's On-Stage showchoir, cheerleaders, and dance team was on tap. Courtney and David were at the choir and Drama club table when David saw Keisha arriving at the high school day.

"Hey, David," said Keisha.

"Keisha!" yelled David.

David then ran over to Keisha, and gave her a big hug.

"Are you having fun, David?" asked Keisha.

"Yes," said David. "I thought you weren't coming."

"I didn't think so, either," said Keisha, "but I was starting to miss you, so I thought maybe I should come down here and see about you."

"Well, you made it just in time for the big show," said David.

"Hey, Keisha," said Courtney.

"Hey, Courtney," said Keisha.

Just then Jenny, Kerry, Latasha, Cheryl, Ronnie, Shanna, Erica, and lots of other Canaby High School seniors arrived at the special high school day.

"Hey, Keisha," said Jenny.

"Jenny, what brought you all here?" asked Keisha.

"We just felt like coming," said Jenny.

"We're all exempt from finals," said Kerry.

"Well, you all made it in time for the big show," said David.

"This is better than taking finals," said Erica.

"I know," said Ronnie. "I am just about ready for school to be over."

"Yeah, me, too," said Cheryl.

"But we still have to get ready for graduation," said Latasha.

"That's right," said Kerry. "Our graduation is May 25."

"And most of us are graduating with honors," said Shanna.

When the special assembly show started, the school's Jazz Lab band started performing. Soon the cheerleaders performed a number. But when the dance team started performing, all of the high school day recruits were really into the show. Courtney, in her new dance team uniform, was telling David the good news.

"How do I look, David?" asked Courtney.

David then saw Courtney in her new uniform.

"Courtney, did you make the dance team?" he asked.

"Yes," said Courtney. "This is what I'll be doing next year."

"Congratulations," said David. "I'm very proud of you."

"Thank you, David," said Courtney.

Later that afternoon, in front of the Fine Arts Building, David, worried about his little sister, was sitting on the steps of the building when Kerry found him.

"Hey David, are you okay?" asked Kerry.

"Yes, Kerry," said David. "I'm fine."

"You don't look fine," said Kerry.

"Well, it's a long, long story," said David.

"David, you know you can talk to me when things go wrong," said Kerry. "Better yet, you can talk to Jenny, or Courtney, or even Keisha."

"Well, okay," said David.

Just then Kerry sat down beside David.

"Kerry, it's my sister, Robbie," said David.

"What about Robbie?" asked Kerry.

"She's happy for me and Keisha," said David.

"Well, that's terrific," said Kerry.

"But she might be learning of what's happening with me and Keisha with the help of rumors going around at her school," said David, "and that, I'm not very happy about."

"David, as long as she's happy for you, everything's okay," said Kerry. "Even I'm happy for you, and so is Jenny."

Just then Jenny and a very excitable Courtney walked out the front door of the building.

"Is everything okay, Kerry?" asked Jenny.

"Yes," said Kerry. "We can see Courtney's happy."

"Oh, she's excited about making the dance team," said Jenny.

"I'm thrilled," said Courtney. "Really, really thrilled."

"Can I ask you something, Jenny?" asked David.

"You sure can," said Jenny.

"Do you know anyone at Canaby Junior High School?" asked David.

"Yes, I do," said Jenny. "Why?"

"Because my sister Robbie goes there," said David, "and some other students are spreading rumors to her about me and Keisha."

"He just talked to me about it," said Kerry.

Just then Shanna walked out of the front door.

"Hey, guess what, everybody?" she asked. "Rosalynn wants to take all of us to a very special pizza party."

Around three o' clock that afternoon, at the pizza parlor in Canaby, the special pizza party was taking place. The place was all decorated with balloons and ribbons, music was being played, and the place was packed. Keisha, David, Rosalynn, two of her friends, Jenny, Kerry, Courtney, Shanna, and Erica were all seated at a table talking about college plans.

"So, which college are you going to, David?" asked Rosalynn.

"To Canaby Junior College," said David.

"Then maybe you and I could have some classes together in the fall," said Rosalynn.

"Yeah, Rosalynn," said David. "Maybe so."

"Maybe we can have some classes together, too," said Courtney.

"Yeah, maybe," said David. "I just haven't made out my schedule yet."

"But what are you going to do about Keisha?" asked Rosalynn.

"Oh, we're still going to be together," said Keisha. "I'll write him, and call him, and visit him. And he'll be able to write, call, and visit me."

"That's right," said David. "I have no plans of breaking up with you."

"Good luck at CJC," said Keisha.

"Thanks, Keisha," said David. "Good luck at UAB in Birmingham."

"Thank you, David," said Keisha.

"Besides, think about the bright side, David," said Kerry. "You'll probably be able to visit me and Jenny at the University of Mississippi in Oxford."

"We'll probably give you our addresses for Ole Miss at the end of the school year," said Jenny, "so that you can visit me and Kerry in the fall."

"And I might go to Ole Miss when I finish at CJC," said Courtney.

"At least Erica and I will be closer to Jenny and Kerry at Mississippi State University in Starkville," said Shanna.

"Oh, I forgot," said Erica. "We have four-year scholarships to Mississippi State coming to us."

"And I'll probably transfer to State after CJC, too," said Rosalynn. "See, I'm majoring in Agricultural Sciences, and so I'll probably have to go to State because of my major."

"So I guess I'm the only one at this table who's leaving the state of Mississippi after high school," said Keisha.

"Don't feel bad about it, Keisha," said a friend of Rosalynn.

"At least you don't have to worry about losing David," said the other friend of Rosalynn.

"Thank you," said Keisha.

"Besides, the yearbook details it all," said Shanna.

"Are the yearbooks in already?" asked Erica.

"Yes," said Shanna, "and I already have a copy."

Shanna then opened her copy of the school yearbook, and showed it to Keisha, David, Jenny, Kerry, Rosalynn and her friends, Shanna, and Erica. Inside the yearbook, Keisha, David, Jenny, Kerry, Shanna, and Erica saw exactly what made them popular at Canaby High School. When they saw the picture of Keisha and David as prom queen and prom king in the yearbook, they were really, really happy.

"Keisha and David made a really, really wonderful prom queen and prom king," said Shanna.

"Yeah, I know," said Jenny. "They made a really beautiful couple on prom night."

"And they make a really beautiful couple right here, right now," said Kerry.

"Why don't I take a picture of Keisha and David?" suggested Erica. "I have my camera with me."

"That's a great idea," said Courtney.

Erica then took the picture of Keisha and David. Keisha and David then posed for the picture, while Shanna, Jenny, Kerry, Courtney, Rosalynn, and her two friends watched. When the picture was taken, everyone in the pizza parlor applauded for Erica. Even though the yearbook said it all, the picture was just one more proof that Keisha and David make an excellent couple.

SIXTEEN

One afternoon in May, prior to graduation day, Keisha and David decided to spend some time at a park in Jackson. They were seated on a bench thumming through Keisha's school yearbook, which had a lot detailing most of their school accomplishments. There were lots of children playing in the park. Keisha and David saw almost every picture in the yearbook. But when they saw their picture of Prom Queen and Prom King in the yearbook, they were really, really happy.

"That's us," said Keisha, "as Prom Queen and King."

"Yeah, I know," said David. "That's what a lot of our classmates will probably remember us by."

"David, that's what some will remember us by," said Keisha. "But this prom thing is just one of our many accomplishments at Canaby High School."

"Oh," thought David. "I knew that."

"Let me show you some more pictures of us together," said Keisha.

Keisha then showed David their picture for Senior Class Favorite in the yearbook. In the picture, Keisha had on her cheerleader uniform.

"That's us when we made class favorite," said Keisha.

"That's really wonderful," said David.

"Did I make a great cheerleader this past football season or what?" asked Keisha.

"I truly think you did," said David.

Keisha then showed David several other pictures in the yearbook, including pictures of Keisha as Homecoming Queen and David as her escort, the school choir picture, the picture of the Distributive Education Clubs of America, the Student Council picture, the picture of the Future Business Leaders of America, the picture of the

Youth America Campus Club, the school newspaper picture, the school choir picture, the Drama club picture, the National Honor Society picture, and the picture of her as Most Beautiful and him as Favorite Beau from the school beauty pageant. Finally, she showed him the picture of the varsity football cheerleaders.

"Now see how much there is in this yearbook that makes us popular?" asked Keisha.

"Yeah," said David. "Those are a lot of accomplishments."

"And I believe there's at least one more accomplishment in store for us at Canaby High School," said Keisha.

"What's that?" asked David.

"Valedictorian and Salutatorian," said Keisha

"That's right," said David.

Just then Keisha and David started walking through the park.

"But what's going to happen to us when we start college in the fall?" asked David.

"What do you mean?" asked Keisha.

"You're going to the University of Alabama in Birmingham," said David, "and I'm going to Canaby Junior College."

"Think about the bright side, David," said Keisha. "We'll have each other's address, so we can at least write each other. And I'll come back and visit you on some occasions. And you'll probably be able to visit me in Alabama. And we might be able to call each other at times."

"Thanks for telling me," said David. "Now I don't have to worry about losing you when this year is over."

"I don't think you'll lose me at all, David," said Keisha.

"I'm just hoping I dont," said David, "because you mean the world to me."

"And you mean the world to me, too," said Keisha.

"Thank you, Keisha," said David.

There were children playing all over the park. Younger kids playing on monkey bars, slides, and swings, while older kids, between the ages of ten and thirteen, were sharing conversations. Keisha and David were watching what was going on.

"Can I ask you something, David?" asked Keisha.

"Yes, Keisha," said David.

"Is this where our kids might be several years from now if we were to get married?" asked Keisha.

"Probably so, Keisha," said David.

"This is something that I wasn't able to do as a child," said Keisha.

"I know," said David. "But at least we've got a memorable Senior year."

"That's right," said Keisha. "We do have a lot of high school memories."

Suddenly Jenny and Kerry arrived at the park with ice cream cones.

"Hi, David," said Kerry.

"I didn't know you two were coming down here," said David.

"Well, we surprised you," said Jenny.

"I'll bet you two are enjoying the nice, sunny afternoon," said Kerry.

"Well, it looks that way," said Keisha.

"What place around here sells ice cream cones?" asked David.

"That store across from the park," said Jenny.

"I didn't know a convenience store sells ice cream cones," said David.

Just then Rosalynn and two of her friends arrived at the park with five ice cream cones, including one for Keisha and one for David.

"Are you having fun, David?" asked Rosalynn.

"Yes, I'm having fun, Rosalynn," said David.

"I got you two ice cream cones," said Rosalynn.

"Thanks, Rosalynn," said Keisha. "Boy, I just love ice cream."

"Me, too," said Rosalynn. "It's my favorite snack in the whole wide world."

"You know what they always say," said Jenny. "I scream, you scream, we all scream for ice cream."

"At least me and Jenny scream for ice cream," said Kerry. "Especially on a sunny day like this."

"I did a class debate on ice cream last year," said David.

"Well, how did you do on it?" asked Rosalynn.

"I did wonderful on it," said David.

"He got an 'A-plus' on it," said Keisha.

"That's excellent, David," said Jenny. "I'm very proud of you."

"I'm proud of you, too," said Kerry.

"Thank you," said David.

"Thank you very much," said Keisha.

Later that night at home, David was fast asleep in bed when Robbie woke him up.

"David, I need to talk to you," said Robbie.

David then turned his lamp on.

"What is it, Robbie?" he said.

"I think you need to talk to the principal at my school," said Robbie.

"Why?" asked David.

"Because I almost got into a fight at school today," said Robbie.

"Robbie, it will be okay," said David.

"Some of those classmates are threatening me," said Robbie.

"Okay, Robbie," said David, "I tell you what. Tomorrow, I am going to pick you up from school. There, I will be able to witness what's going on."

"Well, okay," said Robbie. "That's very sweet of you."

"Thank you, Robbie," said David.

"Good night, David," said Robbie

"Good night, Robbie," said David.

Robbie then left the room, and David turned his light back off, and went back to bed.

The next afternoon, the campus of Canaby Junior High School was crowded as lots of seventh and eighth graders, most of them girls, were conversing with other students. School was over for the day, and Robbie was standing near the gymnasium waiting for David to pick her up when she overheard several girls talking about Keisha and David.

"Isn't that Robbie Malone over there near the gym?" asked a girl in the group.

"Yeah," said another girl. "She's the one whose brother is dating that crazy Keisha Blackledge."

"She'll probably beat him up one day," said a third girl. "She's a very violent girl."

"I heard she was a prom queen," said a fourth girl.

"She's not a prom queen," said the second girl. "She's too crazy to be a prom queen."

Just then Robbie confronted the group of girls.

"Hey, you all are going to get enough of talking about my brother," said Robbie.

"We're not talking about your brother," said the third girl.

"You all are liars," said Robbie.

Just then David arrived on campus in his car to pick Robbie up. He immediately saw what was going on.

"Hey Robbie?" asked David, "I'm ready to go."

Robbie then ran to the car.

"David, they're the ones talking about you and Keisha," said Robbie.

"Hey David, your girlfriend's crazy," said the fourth girl.

"See what I mean, David," said Robbie.

"Yeah, Robbie," said David.

David immediately turned his car off. He then got out of the car, and headed toward the group of girls.

"Hey!" he yelled, "why don't you all find someone else to talk about?"

"We can talk about whoever we want to," said the second girl.

"Not about Keisha," said David, in a state of anger.

"You can't stop us from talking about her," said a fifth girl in the group.

"David, let's get out of here," said Robbie.

"You're probably right, Robbie," said David.

Just then two of Robbie's friends, both girls, walked out of the school building when they saw Robbie and David being picked on. They immediately ran over to Robbie and David.

"Don't let them get to you, Robbie," said the first friend.

"I'm trying not to," said Robbie.

"Her brother's a wacko," said the third girl.

"Why don't you all just leave Robbie and her brother alone?" suggested the second friend.

"Let's go, Robbie," said David.

Robbie and David then headed to their car. But, unfortunately, one of the six girls sought to get revenge against Robbie and David.

"You're crazy, David!" she yelled. "You're really crazy."

"I beg your pardon!" yelled David.

"You're really crazy!" yelled the girl. "I hope Keisha beats you up!"

David, so mad that he could hardly talk, immediately ran over to the girl. Robbie, her two friends, and lots of other Junior High school students were witnessing.

"You're going to get enough of threatening me and my sister!" yelled David.

"David, please don't create a scene!" cried Robbie.

"I'm trying not to," said David.

"Just take your belligerent sister and get out of here!" yelled the girl.

"How dare you call Robbie belligerent!" yelled David.

Just then the girl jumped on David, and started punching him and beating him as hard as she could. David didn't fight back against her, but Robbie and her two friends, as well as lots of other Junior High students, were shocked as the girl was beating David. Several boys on the scene tried to break up the fight, one girl ran inside to try to find a teacher, and three other boys were comforting Robbie while she had tears in her eyes.

"It's okay, Robbie," said a boy.

"Thank you," said Robbie.

When the fight did end, David, surrounded by Robbie's two friends and lots of other girls, had several bruises on him.

"It wasn't your fault, David," said the first friend.

"You didn't do anything wrong," said the second friend.

"I feel sorry for you, David!" shouted the girl that fought him. "I really do!"

"Well, good for you!" yelled David.

Later that evening, at David's house, the doorbell rang, and Robbie answered it. It was her two friends from school.

"Hey, Robbie," said the first friend. "Is David okay?"

"Oh, he's just fine," said Robbie.

"Can we talk to him?" asked the second friend.

"Yes, you all can," said Robbie. "I'll go and get him."

Robbie then went to get David.

"Do you think David and Keisha make a cute couple?" asked the first friend.

"Of course I do," said the second friend. "But why do they have to be the ones to be teased?"

Robbie and David then walked into the living room.

"Hey, David," said the first friend.

"I'm surprised that you all came to see me," said David, "because I don't even know you two."

"That's no problem," said Robbie,

Robbie then introduced him to the two girls.

"This is Alycia Wayne," said Robbie, referring to the first friend, "and this is Brittaney Phillips," she added, referring to the second friend.

"It's nice to meet you two," said David.

"Would you two like sodas?" asked Robbie.

"Sure, we would," said Alycia.

A little while later, Robbie, David, Alycia, and Brittaney were on the back porch of the house talking while enjoying sodas. David was frustrated about the situation Robbie was in.

"David, we're happy for you and Keisha," said Brittaney. "Better yet, we just don't think it's right for the two of you to be victims of rumors."

"I'm glad, especially after what has happened to me this Spring," said David.

"David, anyone can see that you and Keisha make a cute couple," said Alycia.

"Then why do other girls tease me about it?" asked David.

"David, as long as you've got enough people that are happy for you," said Robbie, "everything's okay."

"Besides, guys at school are staying away from girls that trouble Robbie," said Brittaney.

"Then I guess I'm a very lucky guy," said David.

"David, you know you're much more than a lucky guy," said Alycia. "You've got a lot of people at Canaby High School that are on your side; you're a straight-A student; you're in several clubs at Canaby High School; and some of the girls at Canaby Junior High School are on your side."

"Doesn't that make you feel good, David?" asked Brittaney. "To have such a steady girl that mostly everyone sees you two as a cute couple."

"Yes, it does," said David.

"I'm glad you're feeling better, David," said Robbie.

When it came time for the Senior Breakfast at Canaby High School, the cafeteria was packed, and breakfast was being served when Keisha and David arrived. David was not very happy because he was worried about his sister.

"David, it will be okay," said Keisha. "Trust me."

"Keisha, I'm trying to be as calm as I can," said David, "but those Junior High girls don't have the right to talk about my sister like that."

"David, you worry too much," said Keisha. "Don't let things like this upset you."

"I guess you're right, Keisha," said David, "maybe I do worry too much."

"Come on, David," said Keisha, "let's have breakfast together. Okay?"

"Well, okay," said David.

Just then a student that was graduating with honors went up to the podium at the special breakfast to deliver a prayer for Keisha and David.

"I would like to pray for Keisha and David," said the student, "that their high school Senior year will have a happy ending; that their college years will be a success; and that they will succeed in life, as well as get married, start a family, and live happily ever after. Because they really mean a lot to Canaby High School. Especially after being chosen as the Prom Queen and Prom King; Homecoming Queen and escort; and being in several clubs together. I just pray that Keisha and David will always be a happy and prosperous couple. In the lord's name I pray, amen."

At that moment everyone at the Senior breakfast gave the student a huge round of applause.

Later at the Senior breakfast, Keisha and David were sharing a conversation while enjoying a breakfast of pan sausage, eggs, toast and jelly, hash browns, and chocolate milk.

"The student that delivered the prayer really made me feel better," said David.

"I know she did," said Keisha. "In fact, she made mostly everyone in the cafeteria feel better by praying for us."

"Actually, I was the one who needed the prayer," said David. "Especially after all the bad things that have happened to me since March."

"David, we both needed the prayer," said Keisha, "and I'm thankful that she prayed for both of us."

"But I still need to help my sister out," said David.

"David, your sister will be okay," said Keisha

"Do you promise?" asked David.

"I promise," said Keisha.

"Well, okay," said David. "I'll talk to her this evening."

"David, let's try to focus on something else for a change," said Keisha.

"Like what?" asked David.

"Like our Senior year here at Canaby High School," said Keisha, "and how special it's been to both of us."

"Keisha, it's been really, really special," said David.

"That's right," said Keisha. "Soon, it will all be over."

"And I'll be really thrilled," said David.

"Yeah, me, too," said Keisha. "I'm sure our Senior year will have a happy ending."

Will the Senior year of Keisha and David have a happy ending? Will they end up as Valedictorian and Salutatorian of their class? And what's in store for them once they graduate from high school and start college. Only the long-awaited graduation ceremonies would decide all of that.

SEVENTEEN

Near the end of the school day on May 22, the principal was sitting in his office reading a book when the secretary walked into his office.

"Hey Mr. Finley?" asked the secretary.

"What is it?" asked the principal.

"Are you going to make the announcement concerning the graduation ceremonies?" asked the secretary. "The bell's about to ring."

"Oh, I knew that," said the principal.

Just then the principal made the announcement over the intercom.

"Listen up, everyone," said the principal, speaking through the intercom. "As most of you know, our graduation ceremonies are at 8 p.m. Thursday night, on the Canaby High School football field. Seniors need to meet in the Canaby High School gymnasium Thursday at 5 p.m. Tickets for familly members will be handed out during the 1996 Spring commencement practice at noon Wednesday on the football field. Students in 11th, 10th, and 9th grades that are planning on attending the commencement get in free. The general admission is twenty dollars. We hope to see the entire student body of Canaby High School at the 1996 Commencement on the football field Thursday night."

Just then the bell rang, meaning classes were over for the day.

"Is it because of Keisha?" asked the secretary.

"Is what because of Keisha?" asked the principal.

"Why the commencement exercises are so special this year," said the secretary.

"Yes," said the principal. "The prom queen and prom king are Valedictorian and Salutatorian. Keisha is the Valedictorian, and David is the Salutatorian."

"We see what's going on now," said the secretary.

Meanwhile, at David's house, David was watching a movie on television, and was concentrated on what was happening in the movie when the doorbell rang. He went and answered the door. It was the six problem girls.

"Hi, David," said Carla.

"Oh, boy," said David. "I can't believe this."

"You can't believe what?" asked Melanie, "the fact that we're in love with you?"

"Or the fact that Denise Strong loves you very, very much?" asked Latish.

"How on earth did you all get this address?" asked David.

"No, David," said Jennifer. "Who do we thank for helping us get freed from jail?"

"I don't like where this is going at all," said David. "You all wrecked my life once, but I promise you all, I'm not going to let you all wreck my life again."

"We're not going to wreck your life again," said Leandra. "We promise."

"Oh, and by the way," said David, "Keisha got the prom queen title."

"We're happy for Keisha," said Brittany.

"Excuse me," said David.

"I said we're happy for Keisha," said Brittany.

"I can't believe this," said David. "You six young ladies have badgered me, taunted me, provoked me, and have totally made me feel uncomfortable all year long, and now, all of a sudden, you all are sticking up for me and want me to be friends with you all."

"That's right," said Carla.

"Hey, Denise," said Melanie.

Suddenly David turned around, and saw Denise.

"Hi, David," she said. "You remember me?"

"Yes, I remember you," said David, "and I don't appreciate what you did to me that day."

"I know, I was wrong," said Denise. "But I'll never do it to you again. I promise."

"Thank you, Denise," said David.

"I don't even do drugs or drink alcohol anymore," said Denise.

"That's good, Denise," said David.

"We're in therapy," said Melanie, "so we should be okay after a while."

"Well, that's great," said David.

"David, we'll be at Canaby High School next year," said Carla.

"The courts have decided to drop all charges against us," said Jennifer, "provided we stay out of trouble with the law for one year."

"The same goes for me, too," said Denise.

"David, we're really sorry for all of the trouble that we've caused you and Keisha," said Carla.

"Oh, that's okay," said David. "I've already forgiven you all."

"David, can you tell Keisha that we're happy for her?" asked Leandra.

"Yes," said David, "but I don't know how she'll respond."

"We hope she takes it good," said Leandra.

"I hope so, too," said David. "Look, this is really sweet of you seven young ladies, coming down here to apologize to me for what happened earlier in the year, and making changes for the better. But I don't think you all understand."

"We understand," said Latish.

"See, I'm older than you all," said David. "I'm about to graduate from Canaby High School, and you seven girls were ninth-graders this year. I'm moving on to bigger and better things. But I'll still be friends with you all. Even with you, too, Denise."

"Thank you, David," said Denise.

"It's no problem," said David. "I think all of you are very intelligent and attractive, as well as nice, sweet, and pretty. And I'm always a forgiving person."

"Thank you, David," said Jennifer. "You're the best guy in the whole world."

The next day at school, the halls were noisy and crowded as lots of students were looking forward to the summer. It was during morning break, and the snack bar, which was decorated with balloons and ribbons, was crowded. It was a very special day at Canaby High School, mainly because it was the final day of school for the 1995-96 school year. This means that the snack bar was open for the very last time. As lots of students were enjoying snacks, the principal walked into the snack bar, and made an announcement.

"May I have your attention please?" asked the principal. "As all of you know, today is the last day of final exams, mainly because today is the last day of the 1995-96 school year. And don't forget that our 1996 Commencement is at 8 p.m. tomorrow night, on the football field. Have a wonderful summer, and I will see most of you next school year."

Latasha, Cheryl, and Ronnie were talking about college plans while enjoying cherry danishes and sodas.

"Aren't you glad that school is finally over?" asked Cheryl.

"Yes," said Latasha. "Better yet, I can't wait to graduate tomorrow night."

"Me, either," said Cheryl. "Which college are you going to in the fall?"

"Probably Mississippi State," said Latasha. "I'm probably going to be a cheerleader for the Bulldogs football and basketball teams."

"That's great, Latasha," said Cheryl. "Ronnie and I are going to Delta State University in Cleveland."

"That's a good school, too," said Ronnie.

"I know," said Cheryl. "See, a program involving my major is available at Delta State."

"Well, good luck," said Latasha.

"Thanks," said Ronnie. "Good luck at Mississippi State."

"Thank you," said Latasha.

Around five o' clock the evening of May 25, the city of Canaby in Rankin County was decorated in honor of Canaby High School's graduation ceremonies. Cars coming from Pearl and Jackson that were headed to the high school were traveling on U.S. Highway 80 East, passing several stores, restaurants, and a shopping center. A while later, graduation ceremonygoers that were coming from Meridian on

Interstate 20 West were coming into the city. Soon, Magee and Mendenhall graduation ceremonygoers were traveling on U.S. Highway 49 North, passing through Oakwood City.

As the sun set that evening, traffic on Interstates 20 and 55, Loop 220, and U.S. Highways 80 and 49 in metro Jackson were heavy, as thousands of motorists coming from Vicksburg, Natchez, New Orleans, Memphis, Starkville, Oxford, Greenville, and Monroe, were trying to get to Canaby High School for the graduation ceremonies. Hotels in metro Jackson were booked, police were out in full force, and radio station traffic reports were notifying motorists of the driving conditions.

Around eight o' clock that night, the moon in the sky was shining brightly, and the football field was crowded, as over three-thousand spectators, including the families of graduates and members of the press, were seated in the stands. There were lots of news crews from the three local TV stations, plus stations from Biloxi, Gulfport, Meridian, and Greenville, that were covering the graduation. Lots of newspaper reporters were also there to cover the graduation. Soon, the piano player started playing the official graduation song, and the graduates started going to their seats on the football field. When all of the graduates were seated, the principal, dressed in a tuxedo, took to the stage.

"Good evening, everyone," he said, "and welcome to the Canaby High School 1996 Graduation Ceremonies. Tonight, we have three-hundred and twenty-eight students that are graduating, some with highest honors, others with honors. Some will enter the job market, others will go on to higher education. In fact, some of these graduates have scholarships to several major colleges and universities waiting for them. A decade from now, at the ten-year class reunion, most of these graduates are going to look back on this day, and they are going to think, 'This was the most important day of my life.' This night will have special meaning in our hearts, as well as the hearts of tonight's graduating Senior class. This year was an extra-special Senior year at Canaby High School, and here's our class Valedictorian, Keisha Sheree

Blackledge; and our class Salutatorian, David Malone, to tell you why."

At that moment everyone applauded for the principal, and Keisha walked up on the stage to give her graduation speech.

"Mr. Finley is right," said Keisha. "This was a very special year at Canaby High School. And it's all because of me and my boyfriend, David Malone. We did a lot of wonderful things together this year. We were chosen as Senior Class Favorites. I was the Homecoming Queen, and he escorted me. I was the Prom Queen, and he was the Prom King. And look at us tonight. Valedictorian and Salutatorian. This night is very special to me, as well as to David. Because, as children, we both lived in very dark and painful circumstances. I mean, we were both abused, raped, and beaten, and we both have emotional scars. When I was nine, I ran away from my original home in Colorado, and I was placed in treatment centers and foster homes in several states. But since I moved down here to Mississippi and found David, who came from Oklahoma, things have been much, much better for me. And that's why this night is special to me. Thank you, everyone."

At that moment everyone applauded for Keisha's speech, and then David walked up on stage to give his graduation speech.

"Had it not been for me coming to school here at Canaby High," said David, "or for me even moving down here to Mississippi, I might be in a dark, lonely, and frightening place right now. I mean, back home in Oklahoma, my real parents, who happened to be drug dealers, went abusing me, raping me, and beating me as much as they could. I couldn't stand being around them. And I haven't seen them since they were sent to prison in Oklahoma in 1989 for selling drugs. But soon after I moved down here to Mississippi in 1992, things started getting better for me. And things are still better for me. And I thank you all very, very much."

At that moment everyone applauded for David's speech. Later at the graduation, the principal handed out diplomas.

"At this time, I would like to present these graduates with

high school diplomas," he said. "So, Ms. Trina Abercrombie, if you're ready, you can come up here for your diploma."

At that moment Trina went up on stage to receive her diploma. The other graduates, including Keisha, David, Jenny, Kerry, Courtney, Shanna, Erica, Latasha, Cheryl, Ronnie, Laura, Melinda, Gregory, Terry, Paulette, Michael, Larry, the fourteen senior girls that ran for prom queen, and the thirty-eight seniors that ran for prom court, followed Trina to receive their diplomas.

Around 8:55 p.m. that night, the graduation ceremonies were over, and the principal made one final announcement. The graduates were standing.

"At this time," said the principal, "I would like to present to you the Canaby High School Class of 1996."

Everyone at the ceremonies applauded, and the graduates then threw their caps in the air.

Around 9 p.m. that night, lots of spectators were out on the football field congratulating the graduates. David's parents, Robbie, and Keisha's mother were congratulating David while Keisha was being interviewed by the press.

"David, we're proud of you," said his mother. "Very, very proud of you."

"I know," said David. "You all have got every reason to be."

"David, you were chosen as prom king, class favorite, a homecoming escort, and Salutatorian," said his father. "Isn't that something to be proud of?"

"Yes," said David.

"I knew it was going to happen this way," said Robbie.

"We all knew it would happen this way," said Keisha's mother."

Meanwhile, Keisha was being interviewed by the press.

"It feels really, really great," said Keisha. "I never thought my Senior year would end like this, but I guess I was wrong."

"So who do you thank for all this?" asked a news reporter.

"Probably my boyfriend, David," said Keisha. "He's been there for me all along. And don't forget to tell my parents in Colorado that I finished high school big."

Keisha then went to find David while reporters were still trying to interview her. The football stadium was still crowded. It may be the end of high school for Keisha and David, but the real road to the american dream was just beginning. Their college years would mean a lot for them in their pursuit to the american dream.

EIGHTEEN

The next night, in the Canaby High School gymnasium, a special goodbye party for the Seniors was taking place. A special dinner of hot, juicy T-bone steak, baked potato, and toast was being served at the party. The gymnasium was decorated with balloons and ribbons, and hundreds of students, including Juniors, Sophomores, and Freshmen, were at the special goodbye party that was for the senior class. All of the senior student-athletes (Football, Boys' and Girls' Basketball, Baseball, Softball, Boys' and Girls' Soccer, Boys' and Girl's Golf, and Boys' and Girls' Tennis) were all in uniform at the party. The football and basketball cheerleaders (including Keisha and Savannah) were also in uniform. They were the hosts of the party. There were no faculty members at the special party. Lots of conversations were taking place among all of the students. Music was even being played. David was sitting in the bleaches when Jenny and Kerry found him. He was feeling frustrated.

"What's the matter, David?" asked Jenny.

"I just feel terrible," said David. "I just wanted to have a good Senior year, and I didn't."

"David, you did have a good Senior year," said Kerry. "You were the class Salutatorian, the prom king, and you had a 4.15 Grade Point Average."

"But what about the bad times I had this year?" asked David.

Just then the six problem girls and Denise arrived at the special party.

"David, it will be okay," said Kerry. "I promise."

"I know you two are trying to make me feel better," said David, "but I'm . . ."

"So deeply in love with us," said Leandra, cutting David off, "and we don't blame you at all."

"Why can't you all let David be?" asked Kerry.

"Because David's our favorite guy," said Carla. "He keeps all of us smiling."

"Kerry, that's true," said David.

Just then the music was stopped, and the football and basketball cheerleaders then took to the stage. Keisha, in her football cheerleader uniform; and Savannah, in her basketball cheerleader uniform, both had microphones.

"Hello, everyone," said Keisha, "and welcome to this special going away party for the Senior class. This is a special goodbye party, mainly because this was a very special year at Canaby High School. Me and my boyfriend, David Malone, were chosen as Homecoming Queen and escort, Senior Class Favorites, Prom Queen and King, and Valedictorian and Salutatorian."

"Keisha and David aren't the only ones that made it a very special year at Canaby High School," said Savannah. "This was a very special year for all of our athletic teams. As you all see, they are all in uniform. That's for three reasons. First, all of our sports teams have been recognized by the Jackson Clarion-Ledger newspaper, and are among the state's best. Second, all of our sports teams qualified for class 5A postseason play. And third, at least one member of each sports team will be competing in Mississippi's prep all-stars this summer. This is something that has never before been achieved here at Canaby High School. Let's give all of our athletic teams a huge round of applause."

Just then everyone at the special party gave all of the student-athletes a huge round of applause.

"Canaby High School is a very special place here in Mississippi," said Keisha, "because each year, more and more students participate in school clubs and organizations. Of the 1,327 students that attended Canaby High School during the 1995-96 school year, 827 participated in school clubs. And among the 328 students that were Seniors, 215 were in school clubs."

"In fact, we have special-marked tables for the Seniors that were in school clubs this year," said Savannah. "At this time, I would like for each twelfth-grade student that was a member of a school club to go and stand at that table."

Just then the Seniors that were in school clubs went and stood at the appropriate table. School clubs that had marked tables included the National Honor Society, the Future Business Leaders of America, the Distributive Education Clubs of America, the Vocational and Industrial Clubs of America, the Student Council, the school newspaper staff, the school choir and Drama club, the Drug-Education Council, Students Against Drunk Drivers, the Future Homemakers of America, the French Club, the Spanish Club, the Debate Committee, the Youth America

Campus Club, the Fellowship of Christian Athletes, and the Dream Daisies dance team, whose members were also in uniform at the special party. David, Kerry, Shanna, and Erica were at the choir / Drama table, and Courtney was at the Dream Daisies table. There were still 113 twelfth-grade students in the middle of the gym.

"Let's give these Senior students that were in school clubs a huge round of applause," said Savannah.

Just then everyone at the special party gave all of the students standing at tables a huge round of applause. Then a special teenage girl handed out flags to the choir members who were part of the Drama club, including David, Kerry, and Shanna.

"Now, as you notice," said Keisha, "the choir members that are also part of the Drama club have flags to separate them. Let's give them a round of applause."

Just then the crowd applauded for the choir members with flags, and the cheerleaders that didn't have microphones went off of the stage.

"Now we would like to bring the students that ran for prom court and prom queen up here on stage," said Savannah.

Just then the fifty-five students that ran for prom court or prom queen then went upon the stage, and Keisha went to the left end of the stage, while Savannah went to the right end of the stage. The thirty-four students that ran for prom court were on the left, the six students that made the prom court were in the middle, and the fifteen young ladies that ran for prom queen (including Melinda) were on the right.

"These are the fifty-five," said Savannah.

"Hold up a minute, Savannah," said Keisha. "Hey David?"

David then went up on the stage.

"What is it, Keisha?" asked David.

"Come stand by me," said Keisha. "I'm not going to let you stand down there by yourself, and not be a part of this prom thing."

"Well, okay," said David.

David then stood by Keisha's side.

"These are the fifty-five students that ran for prom court and prom queen," said Savannah. "On the left are the thirty-four students that did not make the prom court. In the middle are the six students that did make the prom court. And on the right are the fifteen young ladies that ran for prom queen. Let's give all of these students, as well as Keisha and David, a huge round of applause."

Just then everyone at the special party gave the prom court and prom queen candidates, as well as Keisha and David, a huge round of applause.

Later at the special goodbye party, dinner was finally being served. Decorated eating tables for four were in place, and David, Keisha, Jenny, and Kerry were sharing a convertsation while enjoying dinner.

"David, aren't you happy?" asked Jenny.

"Yes, Jenny," said David. "I couldn't be any happier."

"David, I know you and Keisha have been through a lot of hard times," said Jenny, "but I promise you that things are going to be much, much better for you in the future."

"Well, thanks for telling me that," said David.

"David, we'll always be there for you," said Kerry.

"Well, okay," said David. "Anyway, I need to talk to all three of you about something."

"Well, what do you need to talk about?" asked Keisha.

"Those six problem girls that went harassing me and Keisha early in the year," said David, "they're making changes for the better now."

"That's excellent," said Jenny.

"Yes, it is," said David. "This isn't easy for me to talk about, but they stopped by my house Monday afternoon, and told me all of this, and I've already forgiven them for what they did. They're going through counseling, therapy, and if they stay out of trouble with the law for one year, criminal charges against them and Denise are going to be dismissed."

"That's really great," said Jenny. "They're even here at this party."

"Jenny, they're right down there," said Kerry.

The six problem girls, along with six Junior High boys that they had just started dating, were all sharing huge conversations while enjoying the special dinner. Three tables were being used by the six problem girls and their dates. Denise and a ninth-grade boy that she had just started dating were sitting at a separate table sharing a conversation while enjoying dinner.

"I'm very happy for them," said Jenny.

"Yeah, me too," said Kerry. "Anyone who is able to make the transition from an annoying bully to a very caring and dedicated person deserves a huge thumbs up."

"I agree with both of you," said Keisha, "but I mean, first, they humiliate David and try their hardest to push him over the edge, then they try to wreck my prom queen campaign, and now, all of a sudden, they make changes for the better. I don't understand the nature of this."

"I just hope I haven't said anything bad here," said David.

"You're okay, David," said Keisha. "I'm happy for them, too, but I mean, first, they victimize us, and now, all of a sudden, they're happy for us."

"It's a good thing, Keisha," said Jenny. "I'm happy for them. Kerry's happy for them. David's happy for them. And we're all happy for you because you're happy for them."

"That's right, Jenny," said Keisha. "So why am I the only one that's frustrated about it?"

"I don't know," said Kerry, "but you shouldn't be frustrated about it."

Just then the six problem girls and Denise stopped by the table.

"Hey, David," said Carla.

"Hey, Carla," said David.

"We might be as popular as you all when our Senior year comes," said Brittany.

"That's right," said Kerry. "We wish all of you the very best of luck next year."

"I hope things go good for all of you," said Keisha. "And I'm really proud of you all for making changes for the better. Even of you, too, Denise."

Just then the seven Junior High boys went looking for the problem girls.

"Hey Jennifer?" asked one of the guys.

"We're over here," said Jennifer.

At that moment, the boys found the six problem girls, and stood by them. To the surprise of David, Keisha, Jenny, and Kerry, the guys were boyfriends of the six problem girls.

"Isn't that sweet?" asked Jenny. "They've got boyfriends now."

"It is sweet," said Kerry. "Very, very sweet."

"I mean, that's really wonderful," said David.

"I know," said one of the guys. "We met these girls at Madison Park in Ridgeland."

"Well, I wish all of you good luck," said Keisha.

"They spotted us while we were cheering a team on," said Latish.

"There's a big surprise," said Kerry.

"What do you mean?" asked Jenny.

"They love youth softball," said Kerry.

"That's right," said Leandra. "We go to softball games at Madison Park as much as we can."

"Besides, we have friends that play softball at Madison Park," said Latish.

"That's really great," said David. "Can you all excuse me for a minute?"

David then left the table. In a matter of seconds, everyone at the party, including Denise, her boyfriend, the six problem girls, their boyfriends, and two ninth-grade football players, began to wonder what was going on.

"I just hope he isn't frustrated again," said Jenny.

"I don't think he is," said Kerry. "I'll go talk to him."

David was in the hallway of the gymnasium looking at sports trophies that were displayed in a glass mirror. He then got a drink of water from the fountain when Kerry found him.

"David, are you okay?" she asked.

"Yes," said David. "What makes you think I'm not okay?"

"David, just because they found dates doesn't mean it's the end of the world for you and Keisha," said Kerry.

"That's right," said David. "I have no plans of breaking up with Keisha just because they've got dates."

"Well, I'm glad," said Kerry.

"You know, I'm kind of surprised that you and Jenny aren't even dating," said David.

"Well, we just don't feel like dating right now," said Kerry. "At least I don't. But maybe we will one day."

"When that time comes, I wish you all good luck," said David.

"Thank you, David," said Kerry. "I wish you and Keisha good luck, too."

"Thank you very much, Kerry," said David.

When David went back inside the gym, he ran into Keisha, who was standing in the middle of the gymnasium.

"Keisha, I need to talk to you," said David.

"About what?" asked Keisha.

Shanna then proposed a toast to Keisha and David.

"I would like to propose a toast to Keisha and David," said Shanna, "that one day, they will be married, and live happily ever after. Because, after seeing these two walk the football field together, participate in several school clubs together, be elected prom queen and prom king of this year's Senior class, and then graduate as class Valedictorian and class Salutatorian, anyone in the Jackson area, as well as the city of Canaby, can see that these two make a terrific couple. And we all wish Keisha and David the very best of luck from this night forward."

At that moment everyone applauded for Shanna.

"Keisha, I was trying to tell you that," said David.

"It's okay, David," said Keisha.

At that moment the crowd stopped applauding, and a slow song began playing at the special party.

"Can we have one last dance together, David?" asked Keisha.

"Yes, Keisha," said David.

Keisha and David then started slow-dancing to the song. Mostly everyone at the special party, including Denise and her boyfriend, the six problem girls and their boyfriends, followed suit. The two ninth-grade football players then asked Jenny and Kerry to dance with them, and they agreed.

"Can I ask you something?" asked Keisha.

"Yes, you can," said David.

"After all of the wonderful things that we've experienced our entire Senior year," said Keisha, "can you look me in the eyes and say that we really and truly deserve each other?"

"Yes, I can, Keisha," said David.

"That's just what I wanted to hear," said Keisha.

Keisha and David then kissed each other, and everyone at the special party applauded again. While kissing, Keisha lightly touched David's cheek and jaw. Keisha was so into kissing David that she even raised her left foot up. Everyone was still applauding, and Shanna was still smiling. Keisha and David may be headed for a bright future, but the best thing is they were able to prove the odds that were against them wrong. They may have suffered physical and sexual abuse, but they have what it takes to succeed in life by graduating from high school with highest honors.

ABOUT THE AUTHOR

Quentin A. Terrell was born in Laurel, Mississippi, on September 13, 1974. At the time he could not hear or speak. At the age of five, he was taken to Ochsner's hospital in New Orleans with speech and hearing problems.

In 1982, at the age of seven, he enrolled in public school in his hometown. He faced severe learning disabilities, and had to be placed in special education classes. When he reached seventh grade in 1987, he still had problems in school because he learned differently. In 1988, the junior high principal admitted that he was a very alert student, with an assistant hired by the school board to help him in his classes. While in junior high, he took part in a spelling bee, and gained a great deal of respect from his peers because of his unveiled skills and talents.

In the fall of 1989, he entered high school, and took regular classes, and a learning strategies class. This led to a problem for him, mainly because so many students were enrolled. The next year some problems started to occur at the expense of an intolerant and insensitive administration, staff, and student body.

In 1991, at the decision of the school board, he was sent to Barclay Education Center at the Devereux Foundation Treatment Center in Victoria, Texas. He went there for two and a half years, and his education finally took a turn for the better. In the fall of 1992, he started making good grades in most of his classes. In 1993, he had mostly "A's" and "B's." On December 17, 1993, he graduated from high school, and earned a High School Diploma. But unlike a real high school, there was no prom his Senior year. This means that there was no Senior prom for him. But the best thing is he was able to graduate from high school with a Diploma.

When the school district was notified, they were challenged because of so many incomplete objectives and untaught skills on his Individualized Education Plan. But during a hearing in 1994, reality hit: 'Students all across the country are graduating every day with no skills.'

In the fall of 1996, he enrolled in classes at Jones County Junior College in nearby Ellisville. While there, he joined the Radionian, the college's newspaper, participated in a couple of school plays, "Kismet" in the Spring of 1997, and "The Robber Bridegroom" in the Spring of 1999. He was also voted by his peers as Freshman Class Favorite in the fall of 1997, and again as Sophomore Class Favorite in the fall of 1998. He also gained even more respect from lots of other classmates from all over the area because of his unveiled skills and talents. In 2000, he graduated from Jones Junior College with an Associate In Arts Degree. His major there was English Education.

Terrell decided to write this book that focuses on two senior high school students who don't let a dark childhood past and painful emotional scars interfere with being popular in school and graduating with highest honors. He hopes that teenagers all across the country will enjoy it.